The Voice in the Stone

David Irving

The Voice in the Stone

SHOWALTER PRESS
New York, USA

First Published by Showalter Press in 2014

ISBN 978-0615937533

Cover

The painting for the cover is an illumination page from the calendar of the Très Riches Heures du Duc du Berry done by three Netherland artists, the brothers Limbourg, Herman (b.c. 1385), Paul (b.c. 1386/1387), and Jean (b.c. 1388).

The painting was completed between the years 1412-1416 and shows the household of John, Duke of Berry (b. 1360), as they exchange New Year's gifts. The Duke, a member of the French royal family who lavished wealth on the arts and who employed the Limbourgs, is the central figure in blue behind the table. All three brothers died in early 1416, possibly of the plague. John died in June of the same year.

Contents

Dedication

To Stephanie Zito who I have always admired
as a deeply spiritual person and for her
faith and love for Jesus Christ.

Acknowledgements

With special thanks to my brother Darrel for his
constant and invaluable assistance with the
manuscript and for always being there
through thick and thin.

* * *

To my colleague and good friend Bob Hughes, my
greatest appreciation for his perceptive comments
on the manuscript and for his
unflagging support and belief
in the novel.

* * *

To Ashley Young at The Eckhart Society with special thanks
for his keen oversight.

* * *

I am further indebted to the writings and scholarship of
Anne Bancroft, Raymond B. Blakney, Oliver Davies, Robert E. Lerner,
Bernard McGinn, and Richard Woods OP.

Quotations by Meister Eckhart

The course of heaven is outside time—and yet time comes from its movements. Nothing hinders the soul's knowledge of God as much as time and space, for time and space are fragments, whereas God is one! And therefore, if the soul is to know God, it must know him above time and outside of space; for God is neither this nor that, as are these manifold things. God is one!

* * *

For in this breaking through I perceive what God and I are in common. There I am what I was. There I neither increase nor decrease. For there I am the immovable which moves all things.

….Meister Eckhart

Quotations Relevant to the Story

When I expressed these precious unspeakable things, I encumbered myself by writing these words. But thus I took my elan. And by this I was helped to reach the last stage of the estate of which we speak, which lies in perfection, when the soul dwells in pure nothingness and without thought, and not before.

….Marguerite Porete (burned at the stake, Paris, June 1, 1310)

It is I who am the light which is above them all. It is I who am the all. From me did the all come forth, and unto me did the all extend. Split the piece of wood, and I am there. Lift up the stone, and you will find me there.

….The words of Jesus according to the Gospel of Thomas

Factual Characters

The following characters and references to people are based on fact: Arnaud-Amalric, Bishop Hugues de Besançon, Pope Boniface VII, Meister Eckhart, Peter de Estate, Cardinal Jacques Fournier, Benherus Friso, Siddhartha Gautama (the Buddha), Gonsalvus of Valboa, Hermann of Summo, Pope Honorarius IV, Pope Innocent III, John (of the gospel John), John of Dürbheim, Pope John XXII, Leonin, King Louis IV, Guillaume de Machaut, Pope Martin IV, Matthew (of the Gospel Matthew), King Philip IV, Nicholas of Strasbourg, Pope Nicholas III (Cardinal Orsini), Perotin, Peter of Castelnau, Marguerite Porete, Pietro Rainalducci (antipope Nicholas V), Heinrich Suso, Johannes Tauler, the disciple Thomas, Archbishop Heinrich von Virneburg, Walter of Cologne, William of Nideggen, William of Ockham, William of Paris.

Fictional Characters

Michael Altenbrenner of Cologne, Betty of Cologne, Bishop Cambrion, Candace, Catherine of Paris, Cloudy, Charles Egmund, Denis of Dembreux, Erich of Gotha, Prior Francois, Fritz of Gotha, Novice Gerhard, Giesela of Gotha, Goldie Boy, Gretchen of Gotha, Leon Holzheiser, Sebastian Holzheiser, Werner Holzheiser, Willard Holzheiser, Wurtz Holzheiser, Prior Horst, Inga of Fulda, Friar James, Jay of Cologne, Friar Jonathan, Klauss of Cologne, Knorr of Gotha, Kristen of Gotha, Langer of Cologne, Lenzdorfer of Cologne, Liese, Lillian, Lori of Hesse, Mezendorf, Helmut Ridder, Richard of Salerno, Rolf of Gotha, Rudolph of Bavaria, field commander Schein, Novice Todd.

Chapter 1
Dreams of a peasant

In the Middle Ages the best builders and artists of the day labored to fashion magnificent cathedrals that towered in sovereignty above the villages and cities where the people lived and carried out their daily affairs. An exalted vision in the midst of a society dominated by poverty and hardship, the cathedrals served as a refuge at a time when life was often cut short by warfare, crime, and disease.

For young Erich of Gotha, the cathedral offered a welcome reprieve from the drab peasant world that was his daily fare. At the cathedral you could find town meetings, music, feasts, festivals, and dramas like Daniel and the lion's den, David and Bathsheba, and many more. The atmosphere fired Erich's imagination and fed his secret dreams for a better life.

It was Erich's mother, Giesela, who first talked him into going for he had far better things to do on Sundays than attend some gloomy church where they spoke a language nobody understood. He much preferred dropping in at the tavern for a mug of ale and a few good jokes.

"It's not gloomy at all," said Giesela. "Besides, you are much too young for the tavern."

"We have fun there," Erich said. "Everyone sings and laughs. And plenty of stories too. Stories that make you think."

It was the tales told in the tavern that Erich liked best. They spoke of another world far away that filled him with wonder. And they helped blur life's misfortunes small and great that already had come his way.

"Nonsense!" Giesela answered sharply. "Rubbish and drivel. That's what you'll get at the tavern. You must go visit the cathedral. There are pictures everywhere in the glass. It is like a vision of paradise. You will meet Jesus there too. You can even see hell. You were

1

baptized at birth and so you can take communion. Go my son. You will thank me for it."

Giesela knew there was something different about Erich. He liked to play like the other children when he was growing up, but there was another side to him they didn't possess. She often observed her son dreaming, and though he too grew to be tough and strong like the other boys, when he spoke an underlying refinement seemed to clothe his words. He even liked to go out into the fields alone just to watch the sunset. And when the fairs came through he would spend hours drifting around the merchant stalls staring at the different wares. Scrutinizing the different objects carefully, he would pick one up and hold it for a few seconds as though it were transporting him to some distant place—under the wary eye of the merchant watching to make sure he put it back.

"You have a future my son," Giesela would say sometimes when she spoke to Erich alone. "I can feel it."

"What future is that?" Erich asked.

"It will find you," his mother said. "You won't have a choice."

But Giesela also had a maternal reason for wanting her son to go to the cathedral. He was just fifteen when he got married, the same age at which many of the boys and girls married. Yet just a year later he had lost his wife in her first labor and the child was stillborn. This was not the kind of future Giesela had hoped for. She wanted to comfort her son, but how? Maybe he would find it at the cathedral, she thought, just like she had always found comfort there when she went. But the eight mile trek from Gotha to Erfurt where the cathedral was located was more than she could handle any more. Age had caught up with her. And Erich's father Rolf had no interest.

"The church is not so much," Rolf said. "They always want something from you. They want to know if you have sinned and then they want you to pay them to forgive your sins. That's not for peasants like us."

But if Giesela had asked her son, he would have replied he had no need for comfort. Life was hard. And like the other peasants, he took life as it came.

2

Erich continued to go to the tavern and collect as many dreams there as he could find. Even so, they offered only temporary relief from the sameness of each passing day—mixed with a few hazy questions about life and its meaning. "Why are we here? Where are we going? Should we struggle to build a better life and if so, why?"

Giesela was not to be put off by Erich's indifference. She never ceased talking about the cathedral's wonders so that one Sunday Erich got up at dawn and made the trip into Erfurt.

"They call it the Predigerkirche," Giesela said before he left. "It's done in the new style. And don't look for a steeple. You can hardly miss it though. Just ask around."

Giesela was right and Erich had no trouble finding the Predigerkirche. But the walk took longer than expected so he arrived late for the service. Clustered at the cathedral entrance, a small group of peasants peered curiously into the interior.

Erich paused for a moment, removed his cap, pushed his way through the group and went inside.

"God almighty!" Erich whispered. "She was right!"

The scene that greeted Erich was like some splendid image in a marvelous dream that had suddenly come to life. In the center aisle, a priest, high on an altar place wearing bright silk robes of red, gold, and white, swung a golden censer from a long golden chain and chanted strange sounding words in a high-pitched voice that echoed out into the nave where people of every walk of life listened, prayed, knelt, and crossed themselves. A golden sculpted Gabriel blowing his horn hung suspended in the air above the altar. Before the altar a choir of friars sat in three rows on each side facing each other responding to the plain chant sung by a priest with melodies and harmonies that sounded like surely they flowed from Gabriel's horn itself. This was a new music unlike any played by the minstrels in the taverns or at the fairs, and Erich soared with the melodies as though he were adrift in celestial space.

A graceful row of slender stone columns ran on both sides of a long center aisle and rose upward to branch into ribs in the majestic vaulted ceiling high above the checkerboard marble floor. A narrower aisle accompanied the center aisle on both sides, each with its own vaulted ceiling of smaller dimensions.

"It is like the skeleton of God," Erich exclaimed in awe.

No matter where Erich looked, a new enticement presented itself. All around, stained glass windows in red, blue, green, and yellow told stories of the Bible, the Saints, the Popes, Kings, Knights, Constantine, St. Augustine, Charlemagne, of Heaven and Hell. Light filtered through the red and blue stained glass of the large rose window above the entranceway and the high arched and narrow pointed windows in the apse at the far end of the cathedral spreading a faint glow to the interior so that wherever Erich looked it seemed like he was surrounded by a radiant blend of luminous color. Little side chapels flanked the nave with their own altars displaying carvings in stone of birds, horses, and bees, and small paintings of Saints set in gold embroidered frames. Fine reliquaries designed in silver, gold, and precious stones were placed on ledges at the sides and on the altar pieces. Statues in stone and wood of Mary and the infant Jesus, of more Saints, and more Kings were arranged throughout the cathedral. Frescoes and painted panels told other stories of the scriptures as did the golden and red tapestries that hung from the walls and chapels. Trays and trays of perfumed beeswax candles were everywhere to behold and flickered in a vast array of little dim lights each with a violet halo emitting a sweet fragrance that mingled with the scent of fresh burning incense. And everywhere angels abounded. Angels of stone, angels of wood, angels of iron and copper, jeweled angels, angels of gold and silver, little angels, big angels, adult angels, baby angels, cherubic, chubby angels.

Erich's first visit to the cathedral was one grand experience. Fairs came along at Christmas time and Easter that brought with them wonders of many kind, musicians, jugglers, acrobats, and traveling merchants with canopied and pointed tents of blue, red, yellow, and green, housing small stalls that displayed fine cloths of wool and silk, decorated swords and daggers, jewelry, and all kinds of pottery and earthenware. Yet nothing Erich had ever experienced matched what he had seen at the Predigerkirche.

From that time forward Erich went to the cathedral every possible Sunday. He still dropped in at the tavern on occasion and kept his friends there. But the tavern could no longer compete as a source for inspiration of the dreams that continued to rumble through Erich's mind. For these now came from the new world at the cathedral into which he had entered. And there, just like Giesela said would happen, he gradually began to become acquainted with the spirit of Jesus, introduced to him by some of the other peasants who told Erich about Jesus and his life on earth. In Jesus he found a friend to whom he could turn for help in time of need and for deeper meanings of life through his message of love and compassion for the world.

"Do unto others as you would have them do unto you." "Love thy neighbor as thyself." Was this not the message Erich had always felt stirring inside himself? Yes, it was. These were words which rang true.

* * *

Less than a year after Erich started going to the cathedral Rolf was out in the fields one day and stopped to adjust the rope that served as a harness on his plow mule Bernie. A wasp caught Bernie on the ear and he jumped sideways unexpectedly.

"Hold boy, Hold!" Rolf yelled. He came up from behind and grabbed for the rope. But the mule kicked his hind legs and a hoof caught Rolf in the head right above the eyes. He staggered a moment and then dropped between the rows of black earth he had plowed since he was a boy and lay sprawled there like some giant wild bird. After Rolf fell Bernie remained rooted in place, only occasionally flicking the flies off his back with his tail or lowering his head from time to time to nudge at his master.

Erich went out to the fields when the sun began to set to find out why his father hadn't returned home. When Bernie saw him approaching he brayed and pawed at the earth. He nuzzled softly at Erich's head as he bent over his father and gently turned him over to make certain he was dead.

5

Giesela gradually stopped eating after that. Nothing Erich said could change her mood and month after month she quietly went downhill. Her last days were softly murmured words with a slight smile to her son.

"Yes," she nodded. "You can send for the priest."

Erich had a brother and a sister who were also peasants. They lived too far away to travel to Gotha for the funeral of either parent after they died. Erich's friends and neighbors offered Erich their condolences. But though he loved his mother and father he did not share his feelings with anyone, and he did not tell the priests in confession about his losses. Life was hard and Erich took it as it came. This was the way it was. It made no sense to complain.

One Sunday, it must have been a little over a year after his mother died, a new prior was standing at the entranceway when Erich arrived at the cathedral for services.

"Good to see you, my son," said the prior warmly. The trace of lines around his eyes and mouth revealed a man used to smiling often. "Are you from the town here?"

"I come from toward Gotha down the road," Erich replied defensively.

"That's quite a distance to come to services. You must be very dedicated. I was born in the forest at Tambach just a few miles south of Gotha. My father was a steward there at the castle."

"Is that right?" responded Erich, startled, but curious.

Never before had a priest spoken to him, a mere peasant, in a personal way. To be sure, before this conversation Erich had never spoken to any priest outside the confessional, and he had been attending services for over three years. Those services had all been given in Latin by a prior who was strange and unfriendly. When Erich passed him the prior scowled and Erich scowled back. Whenever that prior was around Erich felt self-conscious about his peasant attire. When he took communion he got in a line where that prior was not passing out the sacraments. Some of the other priests were like him too. You had to pick and choose and avoid the priests who walked about as though they were better than you and acted like they owned the whole cathedral. With those priests, when you went to confession, you just crossed yourself, admitted to some slight indiscretion and left. You would never have told them the truth. They were on the other side, wherever that was, as distant as the Latin they preached.

"I am the new prior here," the priest said, smiling. "Eckhart is my name."

He extended his hand in a way that reminded Erich of a friendly bear without claws. Erich returned a hasty firm handshake, quickly removed his hand, and managed to mumble a hoarse sounding "I'm called Erich of Gotha." He moved off quickly to hide his discomfort. Behind him, the new prior continued to greet other parishioners arriving to attend the service.

The more Erich saw of the new prior the more he liked him, not that a peasant could ever get to know a prior, he told himself. But the priest moved in a way that was different, almost like he glided. And conditions changed after Eckhart arrived in Erfurt. He gave the services in the common dialect so that everyone in the congregation could understand. Following the main service some of the peasants would wait to speak with the prior. They had questions about his talks. They longed for truth and hungered for further revelations.

When Erich finally mustered the courage to join the group, he found that the prior seemed almost like he had been waiting for Erich to come to him. There was no mistaking that the prior treated him like an equal. He, a peasant born on a manor who could neither read nor write and was ignorant of the ways of the world except how to till the soil and eke out a meager living by the hard work of his hands. Sometimes, though, his curiosity roused by tales he had heard at the tavern, Erich dreamed of a bigger world—a world of nobles and ladies, burghers and lords, troubadours and heroic deeds, a world of poetry and books where people had ideas, spoke with big words, and talked about subjects of learning. Knowledge was the gateway to this world. But what did Erich know? His world was a peasant's world. A small hut with a mule, a dog and a cat or two, and the plot of land behind his hut. Still, Erich was inquisitive and his dream of getting the keys to that larger world grew day by day. When he talked to his friends in the tavern about his dream they told him to forget it. That was a world into which peasants could not cross over.

It did not take long for Erich to recognize that prior Eckhart treated everyone like an equal. Sometimes after his homilies Eckhart would take the group that waited into a little room just off the sacristy where one of the friars would serve them cakes and cider. Those were good times and the prior took advantage always asking questions, probing to get to know the people better.

The prior inspired the people with ideas they had never heard before. He said that God was there waiting. He said that you could find God if you just opened yourself to Him and that God was within everyone. He said sin was the direction of the will toward the finite, but that redemption happened when you made room in the soul for the will of God. He said that God must spur you to action from within. He said that suffering was not something people needed to seek out, they only needed to bear patiently what God presents. He said that God is "one" and that those who would find God must become "one" with Him. And, he spoke about the need for the peasants to become educated. Educated? The peasants? With education came knowledge. Erich's dreams began to take on a new perspective.

Erich wished he could get closer to the prior, to look more closely into his eyes. But time passed, and the years flowed by. Had he really been attending the cathedral for more than ten years? And still he was no closer to realizing his dreams than the first day he dreamed them. But that very day the prior's homily had struck Erich in a new way and the words still rang in his ears.

"Whatsoever ye shall ask the Father in my name, he will give it you. Hitherto have ye asked nothing in my name: ask, and ye shall receive, that your joy may be full."

These were the words which prior Eckhart said Jesus had spoken. But what right did Erich have to ask? He was a mere peasant. Even so, though he didn't know why he believed it the instant he heard it. Wasn't God made up of love just like the prior said? So why wouldn't God want to do him a favor? What was it anyway that prevented anyone from knowing God well enough to ask Him for something? Wasn't it one's own sense of wrong doing which everyone possesses? That seemed clear enough. So dare Erich just push aside his own wrongs for a moment, put them in a little private room, as it were, and ask a favor of God like the prior said Jesus instructed you could do? "Ask, and ye shall receive." Should he venture a try? Ask a favor from almighty God?

"Very well," said Erich to himself. It seemed apparent enough that God would not just pass out gifts for pure self-gratification. What must matter would be how the individual could benefit others. For did not Jesus say, "Whoever wants to be first must be last of all and servant of all?" And so Erich thought of the most unlikely thing he could ask for that in the end might somehow benefit not only himself but the world around him. His request was simple enough. He wished to speak with the prior face to face to receive his special counsel about his secret dream which even then was shifting direction because of the prior's own sermons. That was Erich's request to God. Even so, it was not so simple as it appeared on the surface. For if it were to be realized, somehow the doors to a grand new world would open, and in that world Erich would find the way to a life that would bring out what was within himself to give to the world. And so he prayed to God in the name of Jesus for that colossal favor, to speak one on one with Prior Eckhart about his dream. But would almighty God himself really connect with an insignificant peasant and dispense such a special favor? Or were these words of Jesus nothing but a pleasant tonic to soothe the harried mind.

Chapter 2
Erich learns about the Booda

One Sunday after services Erich headed down the path that led from the cathedral to the road toward Gotha and stopped for a moment to gaze out over the cathedral grounds. Two nuns were coming in his direction and passed by talking. They were from Cologne where Lillian, the taller of the two, was the Abbess at the Convent of St. Mary's.

"You see, he is like he has always been," Lillian said. "It was so good to see him once again. He's been here in Erfurt eight years already."

"Hmph!" exclaimed Candace, her companion and lifelong friend."

"You did at least like the homily he gave didn't you? The wise prior Eckhart speaks to us about nothingness. He says the person who does not understand this, in him the divine light has never shown. I tell you, he is just like a Buddha."

"Shush!" said Candace, looking around cautiously as though she feared someone might have overheard.

Lillian followed Candace's glance. A peasant stood at the side of the path looking in their direction, but no one else was to be seen.

Candace almost regretted coming along on the trip, though it was good to be with her friend Lillian and get away from Cologne for a while. But she had been suspicious of this priest ever since she first heard him speak and that was sixteen years before. She hadn't hesitated to let Lillian know her impression of him loud and clear back then either when they were only teenagers themselves.

Yet Candace could only blame herself when Lillian become so enthralled with Friar Eckhart. She was the one who first took Lillian to hear him. The other nuns all said he was a rising star. Naturally, you would want to take your closest and best friend along to be a part of that kind of event. But the brother didn't speak like the other priests. He said things that were not so easily understood.

10

Not so for Lillian who loved every word Friar Eckhart spoke. She too was just a simple nun like Candace. That was before she heard the priest speak. And now look at her, an Abbess of such distinction that different orders called for her on occasions whenever they needed a special emissary. Candace could not resist taking a little pride in Lillian's success and she smiled remembering back. Who could have imagined her best friend would rise to such heights and all because she, Candace, had talked her into going to hear a priest speak. As for the priest himself—Candace's reservations about him were not so easily dismissed.

"It is true all the same," Lillian said, amused that the prior still perplexed her friend so much. "Just like a Buddha."

"You needn't laugh. We've far more important things to do."

At least they could agree on that. Friar Cambrion, a Dominican Bishop living in Paris where he worked setting up a commune, had asked Lillian to travel to Erfurt to deliver a special message to Prior Eckhart. Some debates had been raging between the Dominicans and Franciscans with both sides vying to capture the public's imagination and that of the church. As the supreme authority, the church ruled the state. It alone determined who held power in the Christian world, at least to the degree it could keep meddling monarchs like the French King Philip in check. When it came to religious debates, however, Rome was certain to bestow considerable prestige upon the winner. And prestige led to power and control. Bishop Cambrion was deeply involved in administering the debates.

The infighting was fierce stoked by bitter animosities that burned just beneath the surface. But the Franciscans had the edge with the famous Spanish orator Gonsalvus of Valboa on their side.

"Look at them strutting about, the overconfident little squats," Cambrion exclaimed, referring to the jumble of priests that surrounded Gonsalvus after one of the debates. The Bishop crossed himself and prayed for forgiveness for calling them squats and for all the other curses that had popped into his mind. But Gonsalvus was on the path to becoming the head of the Franciscan order and had been cutting every priest the Dominicans put up against him to shreds. The Bishop was desperate. The debates would go on for weeks, but he could find no suitable match to combat Gonsalvus.

11

Then Friar James, the Bishop's favorite advisor, suggested Prior Eckhart. Not only was the prior a Dominican, his oratorical gifts had captured the order's attention from the time he was a student in Cologne. Now might be the time to bring him to Paris and put him to the test.

"What can we lose?" James asked. "Maybe he can do something."

"We'll try it," the Bishop agreed. "Let those squat bastards see how they like that!" Friar James brought his hand to his mouth to cover the grin that broke out, but he couldn't stifle the chuckle. "Father forgive me," the Bishop continued, glancing upward. He crossed himself and bowed ever so slightly to Friar James, who bowed back. But the Bishop also could not contain a short pleased chuckle.

"How do we find him, James? How do we get this Eckhart fellow here?"

And that is how the Bishop of Paris came to ask the Abbess Lillian at Cologne if she would travel to Erfurt on a special mission. She had heard Eckhart in his early days when he first started to preach. After she was appointed Abbess at St. Mary's in Cologne, her duties often brought her into contact with Eckhart. They had held long talks together and soon discovered that their ideas about education and the direction the church should take were almost the same. They had been friends ever since and their friendship was well known to several orders including the Dominicans, Franciscans, Benedictines, and Carmelites.

"When you get to Erfurt," the Bishop's instructions read, "let Prior Eckhart know he should prepare to leave for Paris in three week's time. We need him here now before the debates come to an end."

And that was the message Lillian brought to Erfurt to deliver to her friend Prior Eckhart. It wasn't that the prior needed convincing to take part in the debates. But the Bishop's instructions also contained a list of the debate points and arguments upon which Gonsalvus had been winning. Lillian was also instructed to spend some time sitting in as a proxy to help prepare the prior for the face-off with Gonsalvus if he wanted. In addition, it would be her task to investigate whether brother Francois, prior Eckhart's assistant, was

qualified to replace him for after the debates Eckhart ᵥ
signed. Where, depended on what kind of future positi
showed he was best suited.

"Buddha indeed!" Candace thought. It was jus
make a comparison like that. The prior would have them all in a
mess of trouble if he had his way. Lillian had been trying to get her to
see something good in this priest for years. She did have to admit
that she had begun to think and pray about some of Lillian's ideas.
Who wouldn't if someone like Lillian was there at your side prod-
ding and jabbing at you over and over all the time? But wasn't it better to just follow the words of the other priests? That was the safe
and sure way. Even so, Candace was forced to admit there was something about this priest Eckhart that intrigued.

When Erich heard the tall, handsome nun utter the mysterious word "Booda" to her shorter companion as he stood on the path
watching the neatly robed pair of sisters get ever closer and then pass
by, he was fascinated. When he got back to Gotha, he went straight to
the tavern and asked there if anyone knew what a "Booda" was. The
tavern regulars mocked him in a coarse but friendly way. Someone
told him to ask the baker Hannah. She knew everything everyone
else didn't.

Erich knew Hannah well. He bought bread in her shop every
Tuesday after work and on Saturdays. She kept regular hours and
also opened her doors for whenever her customers needed her prod-
ucts. All they had to do was knock. But when Erich went to see her
and posed the question later that day, she replied that she knew
nothing about "Boodas."

"Better you come around when my daughter Kristen is here.
She could show a man like you a thing or two. And she's a mighty
good cook."

Erich asked all the people he knew, but no one had heard the
word "Booda." He could hardly wait for Sunday to arrive. There
must be someone at the cathedral who would know.

Meanwhile, Hannah had seen something in Erich's eyes that
day when he asked her what the word Booda meant. She knew that
Erich would be back to buy bread on Tuesday and insisted that her
daughter Kristen help out in the shop when Erich was sure to be

·. When the two saw each other the attraction between them ɔuld not be missed.

"Just like I knew would happen," Hannah laughed, delighted with herself. And she was right. The faces of the pair lit up when they saw each other and an unmistakable flirtation began.

"You've been a customer here a long time," Hannah said to Erich on Saturday when he came in. "Why don't you come to dinner tonight. I'll get my daughter Kristen to prepare us a fine meal. She is the best around. A mighty good cook."

It didn't take Erich and Kristen long to get to know each other. The more they learned about the other, the more they liked what they found there and were eager to let the other know what they were about. That was apparent even after the first meal at Hannah's. While Hannah cleaned up, Erich and Kristen went out for a walk in the field behind the shop and soon were talking like old friends.

Kristen also attended the Predigerkirche. Her favorite among the priests was brother Francois. He was a strong, rugged man who might have cut wood for a living if he had not become a priest. He spoke with a resonant voice that was rough but pleasant and made people feel good. And he counseled with the parishioners one on one just like Prior Eckhart.

"Brother Francois is kind to the peasants," Kristen said. "That is why I like him. He does his best to help. What do you think about him?"

"Yes, he is very good," Erich said, but with little enthusiasm.

"What's the matter? Why don't you like him?"

"I do. Really."

Erich tried to explain that it wasn't the same with Friar Francois. He could never reveal his dream to Francois or any other priest, though he thought he might with Prior Eckhart one day if ever the moment was right.

"What dream is this?"

But Erich would go no farther. "It is nothing."

Rejection registered instantly in Kristin's eyes too late to disguise.

"I will tell you one day," Erich said, rushing to her side. "Soon. But not today. Don't ask me today."

Erich could not explain why he could tell no one his dream. Perhaps he feared it might disappear if he talked about it. He was getting older and all too often fears had begun to intrude asking if he was not just some kind of fool clinging to an unreachable fantasy just because it sparked his imagination and made him feel better. How many years could a dream survive, anyway, before reality finally caught up and put its hard boot down to grind it underfoot? Sometimes the only thing that shored up his dream was his mother's words. "You have destiny in your eyes. It will come for you when it wants you." But when would it arrive?

"Very well. As long as you tell me one day," Kristen said, attempting to tease. "But if you want to tell it to Prior Eckhart you had better hurry."

"What do you mean?" Erich asked.

"So you haven't heard yet? I found out just yesterday. An abbess was here from Cologne going around telling people about it. Prior Eckhart is leaving Erfurt and seems near certain that Friar Francois will replace him. That is why I do want you to like Francois."

"Eckhart? Leaving?"

"He is off to Paris. They want him there for some kind of debates. He will make the announcement at the Mass tomorrow." Kristen took note of the disappointment on Erich's face. "I am sorry."

"It's nothing. Don't worry." What right had he to expect that the Prior would stay there in tiny Erfurt, anyway, he asked himself. Certainly not to be his dream counselor no matter if he had asked that special favor from God.

At Mass the next day Erich sat with Kristen and Hannah where they heard Prior Eckhart make the announcement that he would be leaving the parish for the Paris debates. After the service everyone lingered around and Hannah left Erich and Kristen alone for a few minutes to find out what her friends had to say. It give the couple time to talk and plan. They agreed they would meet the following Sunday at Mass.

"Mom doesn't come that often," Kristen said. "She probably won't be here." She did not try to disguise that she would be glad if Hannah did not come.

"It will seem a long time."

15

"Yes it will," Kristen replied. "I will look forward to it."

Erich wandered off by himself lost in thought as he poked along the path that circled the cathedral. Most of the parishioners took the path on the other side which led into town and also connected with the road toward Gotha. It was quiet on the side where Erich wandered. Only a couple of other people walked nearby and a friar knelt between the rows of plants and flowers at the side of the cathedral picking herbs.

"Ah ha!" Erich exclaimed when he saw the friar and went straight to him. He stood there until the friar looked up, annoyed. Erich excused himself, and then asked the friar if he knew what the word Booda meant.

This was not the kind of question the friar expected to hear from the mouth of a peasant.

"Have I not seen you at services?" the friar asked.

"I often go. I was there today."

"You heard the announcement?"

"I did. Prior Eckhart will do well wherever he goes. But what about my question?"

"You have need for this kind of information?"

"It was just something I heard in the tavern—a joke that I couldn't understand," Erich lied. "A clean joke, friar. I can't get it out of my head."

"A clean joke in the tavern? Who would know about Buddha in a tavern? Best you get this name out of your mind. Buddhism is an ancient religion from the East and it is heresy."

"Heresy! Pray tell me good friar, what it is they do that is heresy lest I ever encounter it I may avoid it."

The peasant's request was highly irregular. It wasn't often the friar was asked for information on some subject, though, and it did feel good to have someone want his knowledge rather than just always to be meeting the needs of the monastery, whether it was copying a manuscript or tending to the sick in the monastery hospital. Here he was with all this learning and nothing to do with it. Moreover, the peasant looked simple enough, though he expressed himself with an unaccustomed refinement that was worrisome. Still, who was to say? To answer the peasant's question might even prevent

16

him from going astray. The fearsome Free Spirits, those strange people who insisted they lived without sin, were all around, as were the Beghards, the male counterpart of the Beguines, those women who often lived in group homes, held their own religious services, owned personal property, gave to the poor without the blessings of the church, and would not accept the authority of the Pope.

"You are certain you didn't hear this word from a Beguine?"

"Oh no," Erich assured. "I know no such women."

"And Beghards?"

"I am just a peasant. These people are unknown to me."

"That is excellent. We must be careful. These are dangerous times and many dangerous people are around. We would not want to be led astray."

They did not fool the friar, these Beguines, no matter how they tried to align themselves with the Dominicans and Franciscans. Playing both sides of the fence just to curry favor, that was their game. Heretics, each and every one. And some of them even begged, taking good money that could go into the coffers of the church for the clergy to use. Wasn't that the same as stealing? That was money the clergy deserved. Look at the good they brought to the world, and all these sacrifices. No, they did not fool him, neither the Beguines nor the Beghards. Want to find a Free Spirit? Just find a Beghard or a Beguine. And besides, what went on behind closed doors in the dark of night with these beggars? There were rumors all right, plenty of them. Everyone knew about it, even the common people. And who could tell what messages about free love these gruesome Free Spirits might be spreading to the peasants? The thought made the friar shudder. Why were such people allowed to roam the streets anyway? Pope Boniface was far too lenient. When would a Pope come to power who knew how to deal with these miscreants?

The friar puffed up a little. Not too much. Just enough to be appropriate.

"Very well peasant. You seem untainted so I will answer your question. First, Buddha is the title for a man. Second, this man taught that if all desire ceases, then you shall find Nirvana. The Buddha lived more than five hundred years before our own Lord and Savior in the land called India. Long, long ago. They say this Buddha dis-

17

covered Nirvana while deep in meditation. Do you know where India is?"

"No, my lord."

"Never mind. You have no need to know."

"But Nirvana, friar, what is that? Is that the heresy?"

"They say Nirvana is the cessation of suffering."

The friar could not resist puffing up just a bit more. He languished in the monastery and longed to become a prior with his own parish one day.

"They call it enlightenment," the friar continued. "It is something they say is like finding God. They say in Nirvana there is nothingness. It is all nonsense, of course, and heresy as well. Have you heard any such tales told around? If you do you must come to me at once."

"I have heard no tales like that, friar. Only the one about Booda I heard at the tavern. And that was not about these strange things of which you speak. But I think I understand the joke now. Pray thank you good friar."

So that was it! Erich was astounded. This Booda said the same thing Prior Eckhart talked about. How could the friar fail to see that? The prior had often said you had to become as nothing to find God, not that the idea was something Erich had ever grasped. But wasn't that the same as losing all desire? For if you desired nothing what would you be but nothingness? And this Nirvana. It was nothing but nothingness. That's what the friar said. Nothingness. At first Erich was sure he understood, but then the more he thought about it the more confused he became.

Erich decided that he must somehow speak with the prior. And he had to do it now before it was too late. For once prior Eckhart left for Paris, who else could answer this important question? How could there be nothing anyway? Who could conceive of such a thing as nothingness? The very concept was terrifying even to contemplate.

Luck was with him that day, for as Erich rounded the corner of the cathedral, there stood the prior who had been wishing the parishioners a good week ahead as they left the service and filling them in on his move to Paris. He was just turning to go back into the cathedral. Gathering his nerve, Erich hurried to the prior, excused himself, asked if he might venture a question, and, getting the prior's approval, inquired in a hesitant voice, "How can there be nothingness?"

"You are the gentlemen from Gotha," prior Eckhart responded with a friendly smile. "Your name is Erich I believe?"

That the prior remembered his name came as a distinct surprise.

The prior took Erich back into the cathedral where they sat down to talk for a while in one of the side chapels. He wanted to know more about Erich, about his family, and who his manor lord was. After a few minutes, Erich began to feel at ease and answered the prior's questions freely.

"My father died not long after I started coming to the cathedral. My mother died a year later. They lived in Gotha."

"Do you have other family?"

"I have a brother and a sister. My brother Rudolph works the land in Bavaria. My sister Lori is married to a peasant in Hesse. They both have families. I was married when I was fifteen to Inge of Fulda who was fourteen, but she died a year later in her first labor. Our child was stillborn. That was, oh, about twelve years ago, way before you came here."

"I am sorry for your loss."

"That was a hard time."

Even while Erich waited for the prior to answer his question, the dream he carried inside slipped into his mind. Should he mention it? His heart began to pound as the words approached his lips. But no, he thought better and remained silent.

"When I talk about nothingness I do not mean we cease to exist," the prior explained. "We could only be nothing without God's essence. Then we would be unpleasant, worthless, hateful. But everything is contained in God. If God were not in all things, nature would not function nor would desire be in anything. God is at once the all, the eternal. God is love. God is within us and without. The question is, how do we discover this? Not just me, but you also. If the heart is to become ready for Him, it must be emptied out to nothingness, even of prayer. Or if one prays, one prays only to be uniform with God. Everybody who wants to be sensitive to the highest truth must be like this, conscious of neither 'before' nor 'after,' unhindered by their past records, uninfluenced by any idea they ever understood, innocent and free to receive anew with each Now moment a heavenly gift. Nothing must be in the way. This is why Jesus said 'He that loveth father or mother more than me is not worthy of me: and he that loveth son or daughter more than me is not worthy of me.' It is on this high plain God gives effect to his will. Here He finds us and we find Him for it is here that He is. So to find Him we must become void of creatures. We quiet our thoughts so that they are not. It is a kind of emptiness. When we are as nothing in this way, then is it possible to experience the nothing of which I speak, the unknowable, the unnamable, that which is everything, that which is universal love, that which is eternity, that which is God which lives within His own pure being containing nothing else."

The prior's eyes blazed with life. Those were the eyes into which Erich had wanted to look, and here they were looking at him, resplendent with joy and astonishment.

"You have heard me say this before perhaps?"

"I have. But I never understood what you meant exactly, and not that I do today either. Maybe a little more, and maybe not."

As though a chunk of stone had been lifted from him, Erich heaved a sigh of relief. He had understood something this day, though he could not put a name to it. And he had spoken to the prior in person. He began to feel like a new man. A man who had the prior as his personal friend and a friend upon whom he could rely. And, could it be? Yes, it was a fact. God had answered his prayer, at least in part, though he had not revealed his secret to the prior. But who is to say how God shall apportion his gifts or in what order? What could not be denied was that Erich had just had a personal consultation with Prior Eckhart himself! He couldn't wait to tell Kristen.

Erich continued to reflect on the meaning of nothingness in the coming days. He felt comfortable with his new sense of familiarity with the pastor, and the two greeted each other like friends the next Sunday at the cathedral entrance before the start of the Mass. It was the prior's last service before he set off for Paris.

"You seem pleased," Kristen said when she met Erich inside the church and they took a seat in the pews.

"Wait until you hear what I have learned," Erich said excitedly. "I spoke with the prior."

"You spoke with Prior Eckhart?"

But the service had begun and the people in the pew in front of them turned their heads in their direction.

"I'll tell you later," Erich whispered.

* * *

Some of the parishioners gathered together to bid Prior Eckhart farewell when the time for his departure arrived. Erich and Kristen joined the group.

"Father Francois will be an excellent fit here," the prior assured them. He shook everyone's hand that day.

"Keep up your good work," the prior said when he came to Erich.

"I will for certain."

"With God's will we shall meet again."

"I shall devoutly wish for it." Erich wanted to say something more meaningful, to establish a closer bond with Prior Eckhart. Once again his dream came to the tip of his tongue.

"Tell him," Kristen said, nudging him with her elbow.

But Erich could not find the words.

"There are too many people," he whispered.

"That's just an excuse," Kristen exclaimed.

The congregation at the Predigerkirche grumbled when Pastor Eckhart left Erfurt, but tales were soon spreading across the province about his victories over Gonsalvus of Valboa at the Paris debates and how it rankled the Franciscans. For days the people talked about little except Prior Eckhart's growing fame. Then they learned that the Dominican Order had conferred the title of Meister on their former prior and they were pleased. Almost everyone agreed he deserved the title.

Within a year the new Meister was rising rapidly through the Dominican ranks. First the Order appointed him to be the Provincial of Saxony covering most of Northern Germany and Holland. Then three years later they named him Vicar of all of Bohemia. Meister

Eckhart now traveled far and wide in the big world beyond—from Bohemia to Holland and from Switzerland to Saxony.

"It is something special that has happened with our prior," Erich said.

"Now he is a Meister," Kristen replied. "Will it change him?"

"Not possible," Erich answered. "He will always be our friend, Meister or not."

"I believe you," Kristen said, taking Erich's hand. She liked the sense of strength and confidence that came over him whenever he spoke about Meister Eckhart. It made her feel strong too.

Erich retained many of the Meister's words in his memory, using them as a guide in his daily life, and often passed them along to Kristen. But who knew if they, or, for that matter, anyone else in Erfurt would ever see Meister Eckhart again, and people mentioned his name less and less. Erich regretted not disclosing his dream to the Meister when the chance was there, and Kristen never brought the subject up again. She, too, feared the opportunity had been lost. Now it seemed like just as with everyone else who ever had a dream, without the opportunity to fulfill it, the dream would just fade away.

But then as if from nowhere the landscape began to shift. It started when Meister Eckhart was recalled to Paris, probably to debate the Franciscans once more, it was rumored.

Prior Francois wrote to Meister Eckhart as soon as he heard the news. When the Meister replied, Francois took his response straight to his congregation.

It was hot that Sunday in the Cathedral that lined up directly with the sun. Inside the people were beginning to swelter. But rumors had been circulating that the pastor had a special message to deliver and the congregation waited expectantly for him to get to it. Finally the moment arrived.

"Time and time again I have been after our former prior to come to pay us a visit," Francois began, gazing from the pulpit out over the congregation and the many members who fanned themselves to escape the heat. "But he has been so busy traveling he's hardly had a moment for himself. Now he is back in Paris and settled in again. Will you believe it my friends? He has accepted my invitation. Meister Eckhart is coming to Erfurt!"

The members of the congregation broke into applause, exchanged knowing whispers, nodded their heads approvingly, smiled, and continued to fan themselves. Erich and Kristen were as surprised as everyone else and hugged each other right in the pew where they sat.

Now the Meister was the topic of conversation in Erfurt once again.

It was the perfect time for Meister Eckhart to accept Prior Francois's invitation. It was summer, the best time for travel, and he had been waiting for the right moment to get back to Thuringia, the province where he grew up. His remaining family still lived there and the trip to Erfurt would allow him to visit with them. He could hold some services at the Predigerkirche, spend some time at his home in nearby Tambach, and then get back to Paris in plenty of time for the debates in the fall.

"When he gets here you must tell him!" Kristen said, with a look of determination. "No you don't," she countered when Erich protested. "I won't let you get out of it. Don't even try."

Chapter 3
Prior Eckhart returns to Erfurt
as Meister Eckhart

Meister Eckhart retired to the sacristy after the service to change robes. Some priests followed closely behind and surrounded him anxious to get in a word or two. It didn't matter much what they said. They just wanted to be near the famous Meister for a few moments. Some of the choir members hurried by. Novice Todd stopped for a moment and held up his friend Gerhard. It wasn't every day a Meister came to town. Todd wedged himself in between the robed priests, made eye contact with the Meister, and slipped in a quick handshake. A couple of the priests stared angrily in his direction.

"Did you see that?" Todd grinned mischievously, rejoining his friend.

But Gerhard didn't see what the fuss was all about. One of the younger novices, his cheeks were yet as red as rouge. "I am famished," he exclaimed.

"Don't be impatient," replied Todd. "Remember we are sanctified always." He straightened his shoulders, put on a solemn face and put his hands together as though to pray.

"I'll pray you, you who could not even get up for 5 o'clock hours, you heretic," Gerhard laughed. "As for me, I'm never too sanctified for lunch, I'll tell you that. Come along now. Let's eat. Afterwards we'll play some tennis."

The two friends rushed off in the direction of the refectory.

Prior Francois waited until the huddle around the Meister dissipated before approaching.

"Splendid homily. It is a privilege to have you with us here in Erfurt once again."

Friar Howard passed by and informed the Meister that Erich was waiting in the chapel.

"That's Erich of Gotha?" the Meister asked.

"I believe so. He attends almost every Mass."

"That would be him. Which chapel is it?"

"The Saint Paul."

"Will you tell him, my dear brother, I'll be there in just a moment?"

"I will Meister."

"We have missed this kind of service these past years," Francois continued. "It's a shame we can't keep you here with us."

"Nonsense, Francois. Your congregation gives glowing reports on your work and you are blessed with some fine priests. I was easy to replace."

"If only that were true, Meister," said Francois.

"I am glad you continue to meet one on one with the peasants."

"It came from you," Francois replied. "It's like I heard you say long ago. We need to hand on things to others we have come to understand through our own contemplations."

The Meister chuckled, and put his forefinger to his lips. "Shh! I got that from Thomas Aquinas."

The sacristy had emptied and only the two clerics remained.

"This will be your second time in Paris?" Francois asked.

"The third time," Eckhart corrected. "The first time was for a year before I became prior here in Erfurt. I studied preaching and advanced debate skills. Then I went there again when you took over here. That was for a two year stretch. After that I became the Provincial of Saxony. It's been nine years already since I left Erfurt.

"Back in 1302."

"It seems like yesterday."

"That was when you debated Gonsalvus of Valboa."

"The Franciscans wanted to get the upper hand over us Dominicans," the Meister said. "They favored will over intellect, but they could not win."

"I would not have wanted to argue that point with Gonsalvus."

"It was a simple dispute," the Meister assured. "The Franciscans insisted God has 'being,' but God is one and lives within his

25

own pure being. If they insist there is something that must be called 'being' in the creator, it can only be—what shall we call it—'cognition?' Oh, let's take it a step further. Make it 'rational cognition.' Is that too complex? God Himself is a pure presence in which there is neither this nor that, because what is in God is God!"

Francois laughed again. "I see Gonsalvus had his hands full all right."

"He juiced it up for us," commented the Meister thoughtfully. "But we more than held our own."

"From all reports you did indeed. How has it been since? Your years in Saxony have been fulfilling?"

"It's meant traveling all around the province, a big responsibility. I traveled to Holland, too, where I was also the overseer. My legs and feet are fairly worn out, I think. But I love to travel the roads and trails lost in the quiet of the hills. All thoughts leave and you become empty of people and one with nature, and when you become one with nature like that you become one with God. It just happens naturally. And then you arrive at a small village and become filled with people again."

The images the memory brought back were gratifying, and the Meister held onto them for a second before proceeding.

"Yes, it has been fulfilling. Quite different than my time spent here at Erfurt. Yet people are the same wherever you go."

"That is true."

Francois paused a moment, as though hesitant to raise the next topic.

"You will be careful. You know what goes on in Paris."

"Well yes. From my previous time there."

"Much can change. Even overnight. With the papacy moved from Rome to Avignon the political climate wears a new face in France. You have heard what happened with Marguerite Porete—and that was less than a year ago."

"The news was everywhere. A very sad case. The prosecutor, William of Paris, had it in for her. There's a strong suspicion it was all religious dispute. The first burning in Paris."

"There are some who say, Meister, that her words could sometimes be your very own."

The Meister's lips pursed thoughtfully and he squinted slightly before speaking. "In the convents I sometimes meet with special women like Porete. The Beguines. Porete was one of them, you know. These women have much to teach us. But heresy? I seek only to be in harmony with the church."

"That's just it Eckhart. In doing that—. Look, you have said that to seek God by rituals is to get the ritual and lose God in the process. You must know that one of the most serious charges against Porete—the one that ultimately led to her burning—was that she disrespected masses, sermons and so forth. These are rituals."

"But Brother Francois! I am employed by the church and it is well known I am opposed to heresy. Such a charge against me would make no sense. Besides, we know what Jesus thought about rituals."

"And also the law," Francois replied, quoting St. Paul. "'Christ is become of no effect unto you, whosoever of you are justified by law, ye are fallen from grace.'"

"That is what we see all around us every day."

"Those who follow only the law and do not know Jesus in their heart, they are also lacking in common sense," Francois continued. "You say there is no devil. While we understand what you mean, there may be others who do not."

"All that is not within being, but outside being is not. Evil is opposed to being, therefore, the devil cannot exist. It is not so complicated."

"Just the same. I have read Porete's book—*The Mirror of Simple Annihilated Souls*, it is called—let us keep that between ourselves."

"Have no fear," said the Meister. "I have read some of it myself."

The Mirror of Simple Annihilated Souls. It was a book filled with Marguerite Porete's mystical poetry burned in the village square in Valenciennes by Bernard Gui, the Bishop of Cambrai. That was before Marigny sent her to the prison in Paris where she languished two years before her trial.

"A strange little title," Francois said. "My brother Felix lives in France. He sent me a copy. That's how I came by it. As you know, it is in French and all about Porete's religious experiences. Felix said the authorities were infuriated that she wrote her spiritual reflections in French, and they let it be known. 'Latin is the language of religion,' they said. 'To speak the holy word in the vernacular is a corruption,' that's what they said. There are some who even say that is the real reason they burned Porete."

"This is a view these authorities need to change," the Meister said.

"You see! It's what I mean. The word has gone around that you preach in German, in dialect, no less. I tell you it is dangerous."

"We cannot always abide by the foolish who see nothing," the Meister said. "We will stay ignorant forever."

"Porete would have agreed. She loved her little book so much. That's why she relapsed after she first recanted. That's what Felix said. He said the court was furious, especially the prosecutor, William. He took some of her writings disconnected of any context and presented them to the inquisition panel. It made Porete look like she favored all kinds of things forbidden by law, even sinful matters of the body. But she refused to defend herself."

Francois brought his hands together and paused for a moment before continuing. "Did you know William is staying at the Dominican home in Paris?" he asked. "It's where you'll be staying, is it not?"

"I have heard he will be around," the Meister said. "Should I meet him I will treat him like anyone else. We are all the same deep down, just at different places in our nearness to God. Some are close. Some are far away. There will be no problem."

"I wish I had the same confidence in people. There are many like William, and they are dangerous. You don't see them coming, and suddenly they have tripped you up. I just urge you to be cautious."

"I shall be, I promise, though I don't think there is much to fear. So I will ask you not to fear also. Some like Porete suffer terribly for truths they possess at the hands of men blinded by ignorance who are convinced they are the most rational people alive. Others go unharmed even though they think and express the same thoughts and even perform the same deeds. It is a mystery as to why it should be so. Yet it has always been this way. Today is the age of heresy. It will pass as all ages do and a new one will dawn as new concerns capture the attention of the world with new crises to endure and understand. Who knows. One day some priest may stand in his pulpit and preach that one of his parishioners caused the heavens to storm and ruin the crops, arousing the congregation to such fury that they burn the poor soul for it. Will the imbeciles never die out? Only God sees that. It is our job to set an example to show the imbeciles the way. Otherwise their foolishness will capture us so that we lose our sight and become like them—blind and filled with rage."

"The blind leading the blind."

"We must never forget to love our neighbors as ourselves. It is the second of the two greatest commandments."

Francois nodded. "The other that we shall love the Lord our God with all our hearts and soul and mind and strength. What a blessing for our harsh world that Jesus said it."

"Amen!" the Meister said.

"Well I shall strive to put my fears at rest. But I shall pray for you nonetheless."

"And I for you. And I shall thank you for your prayers. But now, my friend, I am keeping Erich waiting. We shall have time to talk more before I leave."

"Your visit has been too short. But it has meant much to the congregation having you with us again."

"I have one more service to perform this evening. Just a short one. Tomorrow I leave for Tambach to see the folks there. Then it's back to Paris."

The two men exited the sacristy and bid each other good day. The Meister followed the aisle toward the end of the cathedral where the St. Paul Chapel was located.

Chapter 4
Erich reveals his dream

As he waited in the St. Paul chapel turning back the pages of time, Erich was relieved that no one else was around who wanted to speak with the Meister. Kristen had insisted he come, but he could never talk about his dream in the presence of anyone else. Where was everyone? Maybe they were waiting to pay their respects after the evening service. Wherever they were, Erich was glad they were nowhere to be seen.

At the service that morning, Erich had gotten in the line that formed on the left side of the altar for the reception of the bread and the wine that was dispensed by Prior Francois. The Meister, was dispensing the sacraments in the line that had formed on the right side and Erich did not want the Meister to notice him. After all these years he wanted his first encounter with the Meister to be private and alone.

The sacraments had never meant much to Erich in the first years he went to church. He failed to understand why people would want to take communion every service. If anything, it was boring. But then the Meister gave a homily in which he described the manner in which the Eucharist should be received.

"The sacrament possesses the special potency of uniting your natural powers and faculties to Christ's bodily presence," the Meister explained. "It collects and unifies your scattered sensory impressions and it purifies and consecrates your natural traits to God. In this way God will detach you from temporal things, instruct you in the secrets of the interior life, cure you of your sinful habits, and quicken, strengthen, and renew you with his body. Indeed, you will be so completely transformed into him and united with him that what is his, will be yours, and what is yours, will be his. Your heart and his, will be one heart, your body and his, one body. In this way all your physical powers and spiritual faculties will be engrafted in him, and you will be conscious of his presence."

After these words the sacraments took on a different meaning. Erich began to look forward to the passing of the bread and the wine as the symbolic transference of the bread as the word of Jesus and the wine as his living spirit, whereas before it had been just a ritual in which he took part. But as the Meister had spoken, "it is in being united with him that you will be sanctified. In order to throw off your misery you need only approach the gracious plenitude of his inexhaustible abundance and you will be rich. Believe me, he is that priceless treasure which will delight and satisfy you. Press near to him, and his riches will counteract your poverty, his infinity neutralize your nothingness, and his eternal Godhead sublimate your despicable, corrupted humanity. There is no other way to conquer sin, to acquire virtue and grace, and to experience a foretaste of heavenly bliss than to dispose yourself to receive frequently and worthily the sacrament in which you are ennobled by union with Christ."

It was quiet in the cathedral and the memory of the Meister's passionate words echoed in Erich's mind: "Ennobled by union with Christ."

From a distance approaching footsteps broke the silence and Erich leaped to his feet when the Meister entered the chapel.

"It is good to see you again Erich," the Meister exclaimed. "It has been a long time."

Erich took the Meister's outstretched hands which warmly pressed his own.

"I have missed you," the Meister said.

"It's been too long for my liking," said Erich. "I have come to greet you and to tell you I have been carrying on what you taught me since we last spoke so many years ago. It is here in my mind and heart. I listened closely today and your message reminded me of St. Augustine's words as you gave them once long ago. I memorized the words at the time."

Erich paused and waited for his mind to deliver the words to his memory before repeating them out loud.

"'No soul may come to God except it come to him apart from creature things and seek him without any image.' There," he concluded with satisfaction. "You see? I have not forgotten. These are powerful words and the same like you have always preached in your homilies."

"You have remembered well," the Meister said, impressed that Erich had grasped so viscerally the essential meaning of the message he sought to impart to the world, no matter what the source, whether from St. Augustine or anyone else.

Erich was excited to see the Meister again and listened attentively as he described some of his experiences after he left Erfurt. But even as he listened doubts began to intrude. How should he tell the Meister about his dream? Though he had rehearsed what he should say over and over, now that the opportunity was present, it had all diffused into a haze and nothing whatever came to mind. He began to grow uncomfortable. The Meister noticed and changed directions.

"Tell me how you have been," the Meister said.

"All has been good. I can't complain. But I do have something on my mind." He decided it might go easier if he offered a brief introduction. "I can say it to no other person and it has begun to worry me on the inside so that I will surely come apart if I do not talk about it."

"Please go ahead," urged the Meister. "I am eager to hear what you have to say."

"I have had a dream for many years, though I never told it to anyone except my wife Inge of Fulda, when she was alive, and now also to my girlfriend, Kristen of Gotha. Maybe a peasant has no right…" And then, as though he could hardly believe he was speaking, out it came.

"I should like to learn to read and write!" Now there was no turning back, and the words poured out. "If I could learn to do that, Meister, I could read the fine words that you speak and put down in your books, and I should not forget them like I now often do. Already I can write my name and words like 'tree' and 'stag,' 'sword,' and quite a few others people have shown me at the tavern. If I could read and write I could learn all about the world that is out there that I know nothing about though I dream about it day and night. Then I should not feel so intolerably ignorant like all of the other peasants. Not that I think I am better than they—it is just that to know nothing about anything that exists in the world all around me day after day after day, yes, and in the universe too—that is what is so loathsome that I can hardly stand it. Yet I have endured it all my life. Must this be my lifelong fate?"

There, he had said it. He waited for the Meister's response.

The Meister was startled by Erich's dream, but not surprised. The peasant mind was no different than the mind of the educated and the taught, inquisitive, eager to discover, and thirsting to learn so that it might create. Learning the new was the natural state of the human mind, and, as the Meister said, "if there was nothing new there could be nothing old." It was only the habitual living always with the old which lulled the peasant mind into acquiescent torpor. Yet in spite of the near impossibility for the chance to learn, here stood a peasant before the Meister seeking his assistance for breaking out of the mold of ignorance into which the circumstances of his birth had cast him. Would the Meister help? Yes, he would, for as Jesus gave to him, "Those who are well have no need of a physician, but those who are sick." The Meister had long labored to awaken in the people and the clergy the need for teaching the uneducated. This was the way forward to a new future and a better world. The Meister knew well that even if Erich did learn to read, as a peasant he could never afford to buy books and he would not have access to libraries in the universities or monasteries where he could get books unless he was a student or a monk. This was just one of many problems. But it would be wrong to deflate this hope and not move it ahead. Who knows what the future brings or where hope shall lead.

"It is a splendid idea," the Meister said.

Had Erich heard right? *A Splendid idea*! That was what the Meister said. Now Erich could not contain the broad smile that crept across his face.

The Meister explained that the best way to proceed would be to became a novice which would lead to becoming a friar.

"It will not be difficult to get a clerical dispensation so that the manor lord will have to allow you to do it. He will have no choice in the matter. Maybe you can get assigned to the scriptorium and there you can learn copying. It is an excellent way to learn to write."

"But I am a serf no more," Erich said. "As of a week ago, Seidler, my neighbor, got permission from the landlord, after paying him a fee, and though he is only a peasant like myself, he bought me out. He also bought out Knorr, my friend. Because the landlord approved we had to accept. He acted like a friend, this Seidler, but he buys us out and boots us from the land so that he can charge a higher rent than we can afford."

"That is hard to deal with," the Meister said.

"You should have seen, him, the scoundrel. He dared not come alone, but with his two tough sons. He was not even ashamed, just frightened of what I might do to him. Now I have to pick up and leave the land. It is happening everywhere. We have the choice of the monasteries or the cities, and there is no other place to go. I cannot enter a monastery and become a monk. I am much too sinful for that. And, I hope to marry. No! It is clear. Like you, Meister, I too will no longer be here."

"This is surprising news. And you want to marry?"

"Even at this late age I have met someone. She is Kristin of Gotha. I met her right around the time you were leaving for Paris. She is a wise woman, far wiser than me. We met in the bakery run by her mother, Hannah, where I go to buy bread. At first we thought we were too old to get married but our love for each other has grown, and the spirit of God has drawn us in that direction."

"I welcome hearing you speak these words," the Meister said. "Marriage symbolizes the divine and human natures and also the unity of the soul with God. So many imagine that marriage is nothing more than the union of a man with a woman for the indulgence of the senses and to live for lust. I see you understand true love for a woman and that she understands the same for you."

"Kristen had a husband once before, a peasant like me, but he was drafted to fight for his lord and was killed in battle."

"It is the same story for so many women today," the Meister said. "Many become Beguines. I meet and work with them all the time. It will be difficult for you now. Do you have any place where you can go?"

"Yes Meister. My friend Knorr is already in Cologne. The peasants are flocking there. He is looking for work and has invited me to stay with him and his wife at first. I will set out a week from today. If it looks promising I will come back for Kristin and then we shall marry. She will stay here meanwhile and find a home for Bernie, our good mule, and sell whatever else she can find a buyer for. At least Seidler had to pay me, though it was next to nothing, but I have a little money to hold me over until I find work."

The Meister had listened carefully to Erich's story. Now he knew what had to be done.

"I will write a letter to sister Lillian at the Convent of St. Mary's on Hauptstrasse—that's the Convent for the nuns in Cologne," the Meister said. "She is the Abbess there and an old friend. She even came to Erfurt to see me when I was the prior here. You can take the letter to her. It will introduce you, and I know she will make some kind of arrangement for you to begin to learn to read and write. You will have to apply yourself diligently though."

Erich could hardly believe his ears. "That I will!" he promised effusively. "On my word!"

And if that wasn't enough, next the Meister said that he would write a letter to Prior Horst at the Dominican Priory in Cologne.

"The cathedral in Cologne is under construction. It's a guild job, that I know, but perhaps Prior Horst can somehow get you in the door. If that's not possible, maybe he will make some other recommendation."

"It is almost too much to wish for."

"We will pray for the best. I will leave the letters for you in the Chapter House at the Monastery where I am staying. Do you know where that is?"

"Yes I do," exclaimed Erich ecstatically. "I know the monastery. The Chapter House is right next to the dormitory."

"I will keep track of you through the Abbess. We keep in touch. Now then. I wish you God's grace, and, God willing, our paths will cross again."

"Would it be too much to ask for you to say something that might bring a little luck to my journey too?"

"Is luck something you need?" Meister Eckhart asked warily.

"Maybe not so much luck, but something that would give a little boost?"

"That sounds innocent enough. Let me see if I can find something to say for you."

The Meister turned aside, closed his eyes for a moment to gather the thoughts he wanted, and turned back to Erich.

"You are at the beginning of a new path. Become aware of what is in you. Announce it, pronounce it, produce it and give birth to it. If you remember nothing else from me, remember that God is not found in the soul by adding anything, but by a process of subtraction. To the extent that you depart from things, thus far, no more and no less, God enters into you with all that is his. Now then, my good man. Go your way, and be of a cheerful heart."

Chapter 5
The big city

A slight mist hung over the land that chilly spring morning as Erich set out toward Cologne. Meister Eckhart's letter to Prior Horst was securely bound and protected in a special satchel in his backpack. The trees and bushes were in bloom, flowers budded everywhere, birds chirped wildly, and the tall grass at the side of the road grew green and fresh, topped with dew. At the westernmost part of the manor out across the fields Erich spotted his neighbor Fritz just emerging from the outhouse behind his hut. Erich waved and yelled, but Fritz did not hear him and did not look up.

Like Erich, Kristin, too, was overjoyed when she heard about the letters. She thought all was lost when Seidler bought Erich out. "We'll never marry," she said. But now maybe Erich was right. Perhaps there was a better life ahead.

This was Erich's first trip away from Gotha since the time his parents had taken him and his brother and sister to visit their grandparents near Walshleben when he was a small child. Just a fleeting glimpse of the trip remained in his memory and his grandparents were little more than dim shadows. But now he was on the road once again. He was alone and away from everything he knew. For the first time in his life he felt free.

It was a Sunday so the road was mostly empty. Erich walked for more than two hours before he passed anyone. Finally, a monk with his burro came into view around the bend ahead.

"Do ye come from Erfurt?" inquired the monk as he approached.

"You've not far to go," Erich said. "About two hours or so will bring you there."

"And a great relief that will be," said the monk, wiping his brow with his sleeve and glad to stop for a moment.

"Where are you coming from?" Erich asked.

"The monastery south of Kassel. I've been on the road three days. I have some papers to deliver to the convent in Erfurt."

"Try to get to see Prior Francois at the Predigerkirche when you're there," Erich said. "Tell him Erich of Gotha sent you. You'll like him."

"I'll remember," the monk said. "Prior Francois. Erich of Gotha. Thanks. Where are you heading?"

"I'm off for Cologne."

"That's a trip," said the monk. "I'd like to see it myself, if the Abbot would only send me. Or Paris! Ah well. You can't always get what you want. Erfurt's not bad though for a short breather. I love to travel."

The monk patted his burro on the rump and they moved off.

"Have a merry journey monk," Erich said and waved.

"And a merry journey to you," said the monk, waving back.

The trip to Cologne was over 200 miles due West. Erich figured he could make it in seven days if he kept a steady gait. It was a good pace, but he was strong and rugged and could walk at least three miles in an hour anytime, and usually four.

Since he could not afford the fare at an inn Erich would put in at monasteries at Waltershausen, Wildeck, Niederaula, Burg Gemünden, Wetzlar, Siegen, and Numbrecht. The road went along side or right through the first six towns and the monasteries were located near the edge of the towns. He had no problem finding them.

The monastery for the seventh town, Numbrecht, stood near a stone bridge about two miles outside the town. All Erich had to do was get to the town and then find the bridge, but it was not marked on his map.

"It's just a very small bridge," Ingo the tavern keeper in Gotha had explained. "If you stay on the road after you leave Numbrecht you can't miss it. The bridge is made of large square stones and crosses a dry river bed. You'll see a little chapel there built into the side of the bridge. There's a path on the right just before you get to the bridge that cuts back at an angle. It goes straight to the monastery."

Ingo's directions were on target and after locating the bridge, Erich found the path and followed it to the Monastery.

It was already late and after he registered at the Chapter House Erich went straight to the refectory where they had begun serving dinner. Four other guests were seated eating, but Erich made no attempt to join them in conversation.

"I am dead tired and headed straight for bed," he explained.

After a meal of rice, beans, and a fruit fritter, Erich made his way to the guest dormitory, selected a mat on the floor, and fell into a deep sleep.

By sunrise the next morning Erich was back on the road and arrived in Cologne around half past three. Though the Fischmarkt neighborhood where the Knorrs lived was just inside the city gates, it was Erich's first time in Cologne and the maze of streets and buildings were bewildering. He got lost several times and had to inquire his way so that it was nearly five o'clock before he found the Knorr's place at 35 Birnbachstrasse, a two-story, timber-framed house constructed of plaster and wood.

A merchant of cheap wine occupied the first floor. Erich entered the shop where three customers milled about examining flasks that stood on a long bench in the center and on sideboards against the walls.

"Do you need anything?" the merchant inquired, approaching Erich from behind the counter. "We're just closing."

"It's the Knorrs I'm here to see," Erich answered.

The merchant nodded. "I know they're in," he said. "You have to go outside. Take the steps there."

Erich thanked the merchant and went outside where he climbed the stairway at the side of the building and knocked at the Knorr's lodge.

"You have made it to the big city!" exclaimed Knorr, as he opened the door. He seized his friend in a rough embrace. Greta, Knorr's wife, rushed over from the fireplace with a shout, waving a long wooden spoon. She gave Erich a hug and quickly hustled back to the stove.

"The city is doing you two a good turn!" Erich exclaimed. "You look even better than before."

"Not so good as you," called Greta.

"You must be exhausted," said Knorr. "Come, let's take your backpack. You can wash up. Then we'll have something to eat. We're just sitting down."

In the corner Greta stirred and tasted the contents of an iron pot on the stove that was beginning to boil. A pile of neatly stacked wood sat beside the stove. The lodge was similar in some ways to the hut Knorr and Greta had occupied at the manor outside Gotha. That was a simple two-room dwelling constructed of wattle from twigs and clay daub with a dirt floor. It held just the bare necessities. But the Knorr's place in Cologne had wooden floors and the walls were constructed of woven reeds daubed with plaster. The absence of smoke kept the lodge clean and fresh.

Knorr described how any smoke in the home was fed into a chimney way. "No more smoke holes in the roof, no more smoke filled rooms," Knorr said with pleasure. And now hot water is not just an idle luxury." He crossed to the fireplace and with a holder lifted the lid of a medium-sized caldron from which a cloud of steam escaped.

The sound of sparrows chirping floated in through an open window that looked to the street below and caught Erich's attention. Some tools leaned against the wall under the window through which he glimpsed the descending sun screened by strands of clouds. A rectangular dining table stood in the center of the room with a stool on each side. The cooking area was in the corner on the side of the room away from the street.

"Something smells good there," said Erich moving toward the stove.

"You'll see soon enough," said Greta, shaking the spoon in his direction as a warning not to touch.

"She's a great cook," said Knorr.

Knorr dipped a large ladle into the caldron of hot water and scooped several ladlefuls into an urn. He pushed a rush stick into the fire basket next to the stove, held it there until it lit, and said, "Come along with me into the bower."

Knorr led Erich into the darkened bedroom and lit a soapstone fatlamp with the rushlight. The lamp sat on a small square table just inside the room. It flared and then dimmed, casting a golden glow over the room to reveal a pole with hooks on it for hanging clothes, two trunks for storage, a small square table holding a basin, a stool next to the table containing several stacked towels, a bed, and a washtub that sat just outside a small lavatory room. Knorr blew out the rushlight and poured the hot water into the basin on the table beside which sat a smaller urn filled with cold water and a bar of soap.

"The soap is wood ash," Knorr said. We've been using it since we've been here. It's cheaper, but as good as any other. See how you like it."

Erich blended some of the cold water with the hot and gladly dove into the warm soothing water, splashing it over his face, arms and chest. He washed down with the soap, rinsed, and then toweled off, feeling refreshed.

"The soap is not so foul smelling as mutton soap, I think," he said to Knorr.

Greta announced that supper was ready and Knorr seated Erich at the end of the table and sat opposite him. Greta took the place at the very end and offered a short blessing for the food.

"Amen!" said Erich.

"My favorite," Knorr said, pointing to the thick vegetable pottage Greta had prepared, spiced with pepper and cinnamon and served with heavy black bread and goat's cheese.

Erich devoured the meal ravenously.

"That was delicious Greta," Erich said, as he wiped his mouth with a cloth. "You're right," he said to Knorr. "She's a great cook alright!"

"You just relax there Master Erich," said Greta. "I'll clear the dishes and then we'll have some ale. Light the candles," she said to her husband. "It's growing dark."

Knorr went into the bower and returned with a small candelabra holding three candles. He put the candelabra down at the opposite end of the table where they sat, went to the stove where he thrust a rush stick into the fire basket to get a flame, and returned to the table to light the candles.

After Greta cleared the dishes and poured three mugs of brown ale, the peasants from Gotha sat around the table discussing their future.

"I've already spoken to the landlord about you," said Knorr. "He's got another vacant lodge right over on Furstenstrasse not too far from here. The landlord said if you want it, it's yours. It's the same situation as ours and the same price. You'll have a merchant below you."

"We'll take it!" said Erich with relief. "Will Kristen ever be glad. That's been one of our biggest worries. How did you manage to find something like this?"

"Greta found it. The first night here we stayed in some roach infested hole. The next day Greta struck up a conversation with an old man she met on the street while I was out looking for work."

"He looked like he had no one to talk to," said Greta. "I just said a few words to him. Before I knew it he told me about his friend who was a landlord who had some vacancies in a good neighborhood. He liked me so he brought me here and introduced me to the landlord. When he told me the rent for this lodge I couldn't believe how low it was. It's cheaper because the merchant below has his own home in another neighborhood. That way the landlord gets a double rent. The shop below and our lodge. He's not greedy so he keeps the rent low. He believes in following the path of Jesus and helping the poor."

"So that's the story," said Erich.

"And a good story, too," said Knorr. "When I got back to our little room that day Greta had packed everything and was waiting. 'What's going on,' I said. 'Have we been evicted from this dump?' 'Come along,' she said. 'I'll show you a dump all right.' Did she ever!"

"It's a great story," said Erich.

Knorr explained that the work situation was not like he had hoped. Greta had found occasional work sewing and he had worked a few days making rope.

"I got the job because a guild member was sick. As soon as he came back I was out. Everything is guild here, and unless you can pay a hefty sum you can't get in as an apprentice. The only unskilled

42

labor I've heard about is for porters or street sweepers and piece work for weavers, but these jobs are hard to get. The pay is next to nothing and Greta and me can't hardly weave anyway. The city is filled with peasants from the countryside with more pouring in all the time, all looking for work and a roof over their heads. A place like this is a miracle." Knorr gestured around the room with a wave of his hand. "You should see where most of the peasants are living. Squalid little rat infested holes only slightly better than a sewer, but the rents are as high as ours. I just hope we can keep this place. But we've got to find work."

Erich looked from Greta to Knorr with an ever expanding smile and asked with an air of suspense, "How would you like to hear another story?" Then he told them about the letter to Prior Horst from Meister Eckhart.

"That's terrific news," exploded Knorr. "The Cologne Cathedral of all places! It's not too far from here. Can you get me in too?"

"We'll find out soon enough. I'll be at Horst's early tomorrow, and you'll come with me."

Greta got up, went to Knorr and put her arms around him where he sat. "What a Godsend that would be," she said.

"Horst is at the Dominican priory." Erich explained. "We should get there early."

"How early?"

"How about eight. That should give us a good chance to catch the Prior for sure in case he has to go someplace. Do you know the way?"

"Do I know the way," Knorr answered, proud of his knowledge of the city. "Of course I know the way."

Chapter 6
Interview for a construction job

The friar Jonathan met Erich and Knorr in the foyer at the priory and accepted the letter from Erich which he took straight to Prior Horst in his lodge. After about ten minutes the friar returned with Horst.

"It is good to hear from Meister Eckhart," Horst began, passing over the introductions. He was not being unfriendly. He just cared little for formalities. "He is on his way to Paris now?"

Erich nodded. He and Knorr both felt ill at ease, and Erich gave brief quick answers to Horst's questions. The superior seemed not to mind.

"I've prepared a note," Horst said, handing it to Erich. "You can take it straight to Langer, the master mason at the cathedral. Brother Jonathan will tell you where to go. Langer is in charge of building for the entire cathedral and I have sent him workers before. The guild had a shortage the last I heard so he may be able to use you."

"What about my friend Knorr here. He needs work too father."

The superior looked at Knorr carefully. "He is also from Gotha?"

"Yes father. We were neighbors there for years and I am staying with him and his wife."

"Good! We will include him also. Jonathan will change my note to add his name and then all should be well for you both. Good luck, and God be with you."

"We are thankful for the note father."

"That's for certain!" added Knorr.

Horst turned with a flourish of his robes and returned to his lodge. Jonathan took the note from Erich and went to a desk at the side of the room to make the change.

"What is your name, Sir?" the friar asked.

"Knorr. Knorr of Gotha."

The friar dipped a bird quill into the ink well on the desk, scribbled in the addition, sprinkled a bit of fine sand over the notation to dry it, shook the sand off, and brought the note back to Erich.

"Thank you good brother!" Erich said. Knorr nodded his agreement.

"Do you know the way?" the friar asked.

"I've been there before," Knorr said. "We'll find it okay."

"God go with you," said the friar, bowing slightly.

"And with you," said Erich.

The two friends left the priory and turned in the direction of the cathedral. It was a warm spring morning, but the light blue sky was laden with a hazy blend of grayish half-white clouds suggesting possible rain.

"What a glorious world," Erich exclaimed.

"And how," said Knorr, excited by the prospects of a job, maybe one that even furnished steady work.

It was about 9 o'clock when they arrived at the construction site. One of the laborers told them they needed to wait for the lunch break at 10:30 to speak with Langer.

"That's him up there!" said the worker.

He pointed out a man in a brown tunic high above gesturing to the workers as he traversed the wooden planks on the scaffolds that lined the partly constructed north wall. There seemed to be a problem getting a large block of stone to fit into position. The men hammered and chipped at the block, moving around it, pushing and shoving until finally, they forced it into place.

At the lunch break some of the workers remained on the scaffolds to eat their lunch, their feet dangling over the side of the boards. Erich and Knorr watched anxiously to see if Langer was among those who descended to ground level.

"That looks like him coming down the ladder," Knorr said.

The two friends kept their eyes on Langer as he descended, entered the foreman's tent to get his lunch, came outside and found a place to sit on the ground where the other men were seated eating, and unpacked his lunch. They waited until Langer had finished eating and had relaxed for a few moments before approaching him.

45

Erich handed Langer the note from Horst without speaking. Langer remained seated as he scanned it and then gave Knorr and Erich a hard visual exam while they held their breath.

"Well, you look strong enough," Langer said, rising. He invited the two peasants into the foreman's tent and asked them to sit down on a bench opposite his work table where he took a seat.

"Have you ever worked with stone before?" Langer asked.

"Not with stone, but we come from the land, and there's plenty of hard work there," said Erich. "We're willing and good workers. You won't have a complaint. You'll see that straight away."

"That's for sure," seconded Knorr.

Langer scrunched up his nose into a frown. "The problem is this is a guild job. But we are short on qualified workers right now."

Knorr glanced over at Erich. Neither dared move. Langer took the two men outside the tent and pointed up toward the scaffolds.

"How about heights?" he asked. "Do you like heights? See way up there at the top of the pillars where the archways are? You'll be expected to carry mortar and stone all the way up there on the ladders, cross the boards with it and deliver it to the stone cutters. Can you handle that and keep your balance with a heavy load?"

"I've never feared heights," said Erich. "And I am plenty strong."

"Nor I," added Knorr. "And I am equally strong."

"Workers fall on these jobs," said Langer discouragingly. "They lose their balance. We had a worker fall last month. He was a terrible mess, poor man."

Langer looked from face to face, but Erich and Knorr remained unfazed. "So! You are still for it?"

They both nodded.

"Okay! The board for the guild approved the last workers Prior Horst recommended so that's probably no problem because we're short workers. His word is as good as a pass for your qualifications. The portion of the building we're working right now is the north wall of the high choir."

Langer noticed the puzzled look that came across the men's faces and explained, "that's the altar section where the choir sits and

46

the priest conducts the services. We're building that first because it will give us a sense how to map out the nave and the chapels. It will take years just to complete that. But you work hard and do a good job, you'll have work that can last a long, long time. I'll start you out hauling blocks around at ground level and lifting them on the winch. Most of the men do that chore. After you learn how to do that, we'll teach you how to mix the mortar, then we'll start you on the climbs. We'll try to keep it gradual and not move you up too high too fast so you can get adjusted. You see, I haven't forgotten how it was when I first had to go aloft. It's fearsome on a windy day at first. But you'll learn how to handle it and the men will teach you a few tricks. You'll get used to it. Are you ready to start?"

Knorr said he was.

"I need to return to Gotha to get married," Erich said.

Langer frowned.

"We can be back in two weeks at the most. We won't waste time."

Langer liked the eagerness of these two men from the country.

"Fine," he responded. "You start today," he said to Knorr. "Go report to stone cutter Kindler. That's him right over there beside that pile of blocks next to the pillar," he said pointing. "Tell him I said to assign you to a winch gang."

"Yes Sir," Knorr said excitedly. He ran off to see Kindler and waved back to Erich. "See you tonight," he called.

"So you're getting married," said Langer, turning to Erich. "You won't have much time with your wife."

"Better that we're on the road for Cologne. We'll be together then husband and wife."

"Do you have a wedding planned?"

"No, but Hannah, Kristen's mother—Kristin is my wife to be—knows a priest who wants the money and can perform the service. We can get married the morning after I get back."

"A couple should have a little time to be alone when they first get married," Langer said. "Be here exactly three weeks from tomorrow. Will that be enough time?"

47

"More than enough!" Erich said excitedly, unable to mask his gratitude.

"We start at 7:30 in the morning. We take about forty-five minutes for lunch at ten thirty, and we finish at four. You'll have Saturdays and Sundays off. And, congratulations on your marriage."

"I'll be here!" Erich exclaimed.

Erich took a parting glance at his future work place when he left the work site. Only a few pillars and arches were in place and only the north wall of the high choir stood nearly complete. One day, though, it would all come together to take the shape of a great, gothic cathedral. To be a part of that grand enterprise when just a week ago he had been a peasant tilling the fields of the manor was almost unfathomable. It had all begun when he dared to ask a favor of God Himself. And now there could be no question that God had answered and had answered in an abundance that far exceeded Erich's dreams. For the first time in his life he began to feel stirrings of that great phenomenon people call hope.

Chapter 7
Moment in eternity

It was only 7:30 in the morning, but traffic on the road leading East from Cologne was already heavy in both directions. Postmen rushed toward the city with messages to deliver. Some students followed making jokes, howling, and amusing themselves oblivious to the early morning hour. Ahead, soldiers with their helmets unstrapped at their chins moved nonchalantly eastward, walking along in a loose formation, their swords and shields clanking at their sides. Beyond them a pair of minstrels, one with his lute strapped to his back, rehearsed a show as they walked. Workmen with tools lounged at the side of the road preparing to start the day's work.

Erich's pace was quick. He soon went around the soldiers and minstrels, and then passed a group of monks and sisters.

"Look at him go!" one of the minstrels called. "He'll wear himself out before the morning's out." The others laughed.

The travelers from the city were all journeying to a variety of destinations, castles, manors, monasteries, and towns. Those traveling any distance were usually headed for the larger cities that lay South, like Frankfurt or Mannheim.

The traffic soon thinned on the road toward Erfurt. Erich estimated it would take eight or nine hours to reach his first stop at the Numbrecht Monastery.

For the first few miles the road was wide and partially stone paved, but about an hour and a half out of Cologne it began to narrow and gradually gave way to gravel and then dirt. The day was peaceful and Erich traveled on hour upon hour lost in daydreams about the recent turn of events. Kristen would soon be his wife and in less than a month he would be learning a new trade in Cologne. He wondered if Kristen had found a home for old Bernie. He'd miss the mule, and they had both agreed they would not leave Bernie behind if they could not find a good home where someone would love and care for him. Fortunately, Hannah had agreed to keep him if it turned out they could not find anyone.

Only a few travelers passed Erich on their journey toward Cologne. When that happened they stopped to exchange greetings, glad for the chance to share a small portion of their lives with a stranger for a moment in the silence of the wilderness that spread around them.

Sometimes the road disappeared entirely where storms had washed it away. If no one was visible in the distance to mark the road's continuance, Erich had to be wary in finding where the road picked up again so not to lose his way in the unfamiliar terrain, a happening that could have disastrous consequences in unexplored territories of thickets, woods, wild boars, and bears. Erich shivered. A boar he could handle—at least scare it off, maybe. But a bear?

As Erich watched the spiral flight of a hawk above, it was as if just the outline of his body trudged along the dusty trail, a small speck on a sliver of road in a vast mountainous landscape, moving along like an ant beneath the giant, white clouds that towered overhead shadowed with gold from the rays of the sun. Then it seemed as though even the traces of his outline disappeared along with his thoughts as he continued to focus on the diminishing dot of the soaring hawk which slowly vanished into the bright, light blue sky. Suddenly a sense of eternity filled the landscape with an all encompassing love that touched everything as far as the eye could see. Time stood still.

"My word!" Erich exclaimed to himself. "There is no death in this place." This was eternity, here and now, which was everywhere to behold in sublime serenity, in every pore and grain of all existing things, each expressing in some unfathomable way its own inherent nature, the rocks, the trees, the hills themselves all infused with a sense which filled the self with the inescapable knowledge that this was God.

"There is a God!" Erich exclaimed in absolute wonder. "There is a God!" This was the living proof from which all doubt fled.

Erich's thoughts soon returned and when they did he could not find that marvelous place where eternity had just been present, though he was still filled with the leftovers of its all-pervasive love. The moment in which his focus on the soaring hawk had emptied himself of himself to become one with all nature had passed and was now utterly incomprehensible. No matter how he tried to find what he had just experienced, it was gone. Whatever it was could only be found in the absolute present where there was no past and no future, in that place where time stands still and only now exists. Could this place have been the nothingness of which the Meister spoke?

Erich walked steadily along at an even pace lost in his reveries. He felt no fatigue and no need to take even a short break. He was a peasant and he had nothing. But the blessings of life had been good. He had found confidence. He had found hope. And he had just experienced that profound love that stood beyond all words, that once touched could only increase and would continue to increase until it had touched everything in life that he would ever experience. Could it have been that, as the Meister had described in his sermons, he had just received some small portion of God's own power and might?

The words of the Meister came to mind when he said, where the soul is, there is God, and where God is, there is the soul. These were the kinds of things St. Paul had spoken about, the Meister explained, when he wrote "I can do all things through Christ which strengtheneth me." And, said the Meister, when that happens the soul neither works, nor knows, nor loves, but rather it is God Himself who through the soul works and knows and loves. And, once received from God, the soul is able to do anything.

At long last Erich saw the towers and spires of Castle Numbrecht in the distance off to his right extending above the trees in the woods that ran nearly parallel to the road. It was the landmark he had been waiting for. When he arrived at the crest of the next hill he would be able to see the bridge on the road below and the path just beyond it on his left that cut back to the Numbrecht monastery. Even the little town of Numbrecht would be visible in the distance not too far away. Erich was ahead of time and would reach the monastery in plenty of time to register as a guest. The sun was already low in the sky and darkness would soon fall as though a giant curtain was descending, closing off the past in preparation for the new life that for Erich and Kristen was about to begin.

Chapter 8
Erich meets the Abbess;
The metamorphosis of Lillian;
The heresy investigator

Shortly after Erich and Kristin were settled in their new lodgings on Furstenstrasse, they inquired where St. Mary's Convent was located. It was time for Erich to go to see the Abbess and put his dream to the test. Kristen checked again and again as he prepared to leave to make certain that he looked his best and did not forget to take the Meister's letter with him.

"Don't forget to tell her that you know the Meister personally, if you need to," Kristen said, fluffing out his tunic so that it did not bind too tightly at the waist.

"I'll tell her," Erich assured.

"And remember, you'll work hard. Don't be afraid to say it."

Erich nodded. "I won't. I promise."

At the Convent Erich found the guest house and entered where he was greeted by a nun assigned to meet guests and attend to their needs. She inquired into the nature of Erich's visit and listened attentively as he stated his purpose. The nun nodded her approval and asked Erich to follow her as she led him up a spiral staircase to the second floor and then guided him through several passageways until they came to the reception area of the Abbess' quarters.

The tall, slender and attractive Abbess who came out to greet Erich could not have been more than four or five years older than he. Several nuns who had been waiting at the side of the room spied the Abbess before she reached Erich and swarmed around her with an array of requests and demands. The Abbess Lillian took enormous pride in the little world that had been put in her charge and dismissed the women's supplications with determined efficiency, snapping out replies and directions with a commanding air acquired from a well-honed sense of self-esteem. Her every movement and gesture conveyed strength and vitality.

The Abbess apologized for the interruption, took the letter Erich handed her, saw that it was from Meister Eckhart, and invited Erich into her private quarters. She asked him to be seated while she went to the window and parted the drapes there to read the letter in the mid-morning light. A hive of nuns coming and going bustled across the convent grounds below and swirled around the periphery of her vision as she read. Most of the women wore long black or white tunics.

Lillian was impressed as she read the Meister's recommendation. Erich was not the first peasant he had sent to her for help. How to lift the peasants from their rut of ignorance had often been a topic she and the Meister had discussed whenever he visited St. Mary's in Cologne.

"The authorities would tell us that we ought not talk about our learning to the untaught," the Meister said. "But to this I say that if we are not to teach people who have not been taught no one will ever be taught. For that is why we teach the untaught, so that they may be changed from uninstructed into instructed."

"Of course!" Lillian exclaimed. It was such a simple concept how could anyone see it differently? And, Lillian had been quick to add, instruction like this would surely help eliminate poverty.

But the teaching had to take place under the roof of the church, and most of the peasants had little interest in going to the church for instruction. Nor did anyone do much to foster their curiosity. Only a few of the peasants ever interned as a monk or a nun, and just a portion of those who did learned much more than a smattering of how to read and write. The monasteries were no place for the progressive views like those held by the Abbess Lillian anyway, convinced as she was that the monasteries were part of a larger network of purposeful ambivalence that was responsible for keeping the peasants in their miserable condition. How did you tackle that problem? Yes, the authorities were suspicious of learning all right. It was a challenge to their authority and prestige. They wanted to keep their learning to themselves for learning meant knowledge. And with knowledge came control and power. Why educate the masses from which threats to authority were certain to rise? These were the thoughts that paraded through Lillian's mind as she read Meister Eckhart's letter.

Lillian turned from the window, crossed the room, and handed the letter back to Erich.

"Tell me about yourself."

But Erich was staring straight at Lillian, a surprised look on his face. "Pardon me, good sister. I have seen you before."

"Is that right? Where would that have been?"

"You were talking to another nun. It was in Erfurt. You were talking about Booda."

"Buddha?"

"You said that someone was like a Booda. I searched high and low to find out the meaning of the word."

"Extraordinary!" I was in Erfurt for a few days, but that was several years ago. You overheard me talking? And you remember that? I should have been more careful with my choice of words."

"I'm glad you were not. It led me to speak with Prior Eckhart in person. If I had not heard you speak about a Booda I would not be here today!"

"That is remarkable! But you must be careful when you use this word. It could lead you into trouble."

"I could tell it was a dangerous word from the way the friar spoke who explained who Booda was. You need have no fear. I know when to speak and when to keep silent."

Lillian was astounded. Here stood one peasant before her who possessed a genuine sense of curiosity about the world. From the Meister's letter it was apparent he was groping desperately for direction just as she had done before she found her way. The peasant also seemed to have an innate understanding of matters of considerable depth, and, added to that, he came to her recommended by Meister Eckhart. Lillian resolved right there that she would personally supervise Erich's instruction.

* * *

It was many years before when Candace invited her friend Lillian to attend a special service. A priest would speak who had been gathering fame with each passing day.

"They say he is brilliant," Candace said. "He draws these huge crowds. You must come with me to hear him."

"Is this the one you've been telling me about who says that God gives to all creatures alike?" Lillian asked. "Including women?"

"He is the one."

"I'll have to hear that to believe it," Lillian said skeptically.

"He is very popular with the women," Candace continued.

"Not another one of those."

"All the sisters are swooning," Candace said, ignoring Lillian's comment. "Some whisper he is a mystic. It could be. Something must be going on when the Beguine women flock to hear him like they do. You know how they love anything with a hint of the mystical. Now his talks are so packed you can hardly get in. This is a real chance."

But it would take more than a growing reputation to convince Lillian of some cleric's value. Like so many orphans, her parents had deposited her on the doorsteps of the Convent at St. Mary's during a famine. She was only six at the time and she cried a lot at first. Then she met Candace who became her first friend. Candace was just a year older, and they had been inseparable ever since. But Lillian did not become much interested in spiritual matters during her growing up days like Candace and many of the other sisters. She just did not believe in some silly god in the sky to which people constantly knelt and prayed seeking forgiveness. Where was her mother and father if this god was so wonderful? And she especially disliked the bishops and priests who insisted the people obey them. They were always filling the people with guilt and threatening and punishing everyone on behalf of their god in the sky whose guardians they proclaimed they were. Lillian longed to tell Candace how she felt, but should she challenge the faith that meant so much to her dear friend? Then there was the matter that if the story ever did get out about how she regarded the god of the church and its guardians it would not take long for them to come pounding at her door. Though she was only sixteen she understood the dangers of her times. It was wise to keep such thinking as Lillian thought to herself when it came to ecclesiastical matters. Far better to pretend not to see what one plainly did see and hope the habit would not eventually render one unable to see the truth of a thing at all.

The tales Candace told about the priest had aroused Lillian's curiosity though. She wanted to see for herself if what everyone said about this priest was true or not. They said that he had grown up attending the Dominican monastery in Erfurt which was near to his home in Tambach. There, he was so bright that the priests in the monastery sent him to Cologne where he quickly became the best of the young masters and was soon outmatching his superiors.

"Where will he speak?" Lillian asked.

"Here at St. Mary's"

"All right! I will go with you."

"We can go early and get right up to the front," Candace said, excitedly. "We won't want to miss getting a seat."

The service was held in the main chapel. True to sister Candace's expectations, it was filling up by the time she and Lillian arrived. They were fortunate to find a place in the twelfth row. Nuns in black habit chattering animatedly away had already occupied a good portion of the chapel. Only a few of the nuns had put on the wimple, the white headdress of cloth worn over the head and around the neck and ears which was touted by ladies of the nobility and was becoming popular with the nuns. Candace wore one and wanted Lillian to try one too, but she refused, preferring to wear only a simple white tunic with a slim blue-corded rope for a belt.

"It is much too pretentious," Lillian said of the wimple.

Quite a few in the crowd were veiled and wore hooded gray robes. These were the Beguine women.

"Good that we got here early as we did," Candace murmured.

"Look at all the Beguine women," Lillian said amazed.

"Just like I told you. They love anything with even the dimmest hint of the mystical."

Those in charge of officiating the service gradually made their way to the front. A pulpit sat on a raised platform facing the audience. Sisters in scarlet robes made up the choir that occupied the rear of the dais behind the pulpit. They whispered affably to one another aware that they were a focus of attention. Lillian did not see him enter, but at some point she noticed a man in a purple robe lined with black velvet sitting beside the Abbess on the first row facing the platform. The sisters seated in the rows ahead of Lillian stretched to the side in an effort to get a better look at him. Lillian and Candice, too, tried to get a better glimpse.

The service began with an a cappella choir piece by the composer Leonin. Lillian did not like the hollow sound of the music and was glad when it ended. Next the Abbess stood, turned to face the crowd, and made a few introductory remarks. With the audience breaking into applause, pastor Eckhart rose and shook the Abbess' hand. He climbed the steps of the platform and took his place behind the pulpit framed by the choir of sisters behind.

The auditorium went silent as the priest began to speak in a solid, reassuring voice that belied his youth. Lillian could have sworn a glow radiated from his eyes and face. And almost as if to confirm her impression, the priest began by speaking of the spark of God that was within every person and united each person with God.

"The spark of God within each person," Lillian repeated to herself. Could it be? Why it would mean that He is within, not a separate God outside of ourselves located somewhere up in the sky looking down like some white-bearded great grandfather.

"It makes perfect sense," Lillian gasped, almost out loud. She did not know quite why it made sense, but it did. It was like the still quiet voice within. You just knew it was there no matter what anyone said, and you knew it spoke the truth.

Lillian was not the only person in the hall who gasped. At the back of the hall concealed behind some dark green drapes that covered the stained glass windows there, stood Willard Holzheiser. Like pastor Eckhart, he too had captured the attention of his superiors. But there all similarities ceased. For Willard Holzheiser was employed as an inspector in the Inquisitor's Investigative Division for Heresy at the Office of the Inquisition. Newly married with a newborn son, Holzheiser was ambitious and anxious to make a mark for himself. Like his father and grandfather and other priests of the day, Willard had married after taking holy orders in spite of the Lateran councils' decree against clerical marriage back in the 12th century. While the marriage of priests was strongly discouraged by the church, Willard regarded it as of little consequence. His personal future as he saw it would only modestly require his participation in priestly functions anyway. And now he had a beautiful new son. That was evidence enough, Willard insisted whenever he argued the point with other clerics, that the church should drop its opposition to the marriage of priests.

It was the depth of his abhorrence of heresy that had caught the eye of the Inquisitor General himself, Denis of Dembreux. In fact, Dembreux was the one who had sent Holzheiser to the convent that day certain that the priest speaking there would entertain his young inspector with a most unorthodox message. And to Dembreux, Holzheiser was not just an ordinary inspector. He even came with a letter written on his behalf by Pope Nicholas III himself. Of course, Holzheiser's father had been a counsel for the Pope, but even so, Denis was grooming Holzehieser along. Stories had been circulating about the priest Eckhart, and it would be good training to have his protégé there to observe the proceedings and prepare a report afterwards.

From Holzheiser's standpoint the visit to St. Mary's was another opportunity to further impress the Inquisitor General and he intended to be at his best. When Holzheiser heard with his own ears pastor Eckhart speak about a spark of God that was within each and every person, the fibers in his brain began to vibrate, he was certain, like the strings of a zither.

"Do not think that saintliness comes from occupation," Eckhart continued. "It depends rather on what one is. To seek God by rituals is to get the ritual and lose God in the process."

Lillian glanced sideways at Candace who, as a matter of routine, was even then citing the Rosary which she held in her hands as she counted the paternoster beads. "Hail, full of grace, the Lord is with thee: blessed art thou among women and blessed is the fruit of thy womb." Lillian knew that Candace found sanctification, consolation, and salvation in the recitation of the Rosary. She saw, though, like the priest had just preached, that empty participation in ritual without devotion and contemplation could bring only emptiness.

Like he had stated, "it depends rather on what one is." With the right intentions, as Lillian would hear pastor Eckhart himself acknowledge once she got to know him, rituals like the sacraments, when used rightly could form a bridge to God Himself. The intention of the participant was what mattered. For as Eckhart would say, "One 'Hail Mary' uttered sincerely is more potent and better than a thousand uttered mechanically, for the heart is not made pure by prayer but rather prayer is made pure by the pure heart."

Candace felt her friend's gaze and she released the beads into her lap as she resolved to pay closer attention to what the priest was saying.

"If you would find God, remember that the eye with which I see God is the eye with which God sees me," Eckhart continued.

Lillian grasped Candace's arm with both hands as she took in Eckhart's words. This man was talking about something almost incomprehensible, yet quite remarkable. Again he was saying that God was within us, that we are one with God.

Willard Holzheiser continued to take in the priest's words too. When he heard him say "the eye with which I see God is the eye with which God sees me," the hair on his neck rose and he began to sweat. Here stood another one of those apostles of light right before him spewing out his filthy heresy without a tinge of regret! Apparently he was already popular enough to get away with saying anything he wanted!

"People say that only acquiring ever more knowledge will lead them to God's door," the pastor continued. "I say knowledge is a thing and that all things must be left behind to find God. It is why Christ says, 'Whosoever loves another more than me and is attached to father and mother and many other things, is not worthy of me.' Even these must be laid aside.

"Do not think, my friends, that I am blessing ignorance. In fact, you may rightfully say, 'if you abandon knowledge, this leads only to ignorance and where there is ignorance there is error and vanity. The ignorant person is brutal. He is an ass and a fool, as long as he remains ignorant.' And you would be right. To be sure, it is from knowledge that one may achieve the understanding to withdraw into this passivity of which I speak. And it is by reason of such understanding that we learn that we can become perfect by what happens to us rather than by what we do.

"To accomplish this inward act a person must withdraw all of his soul's agents, as it were, into a corner of the soul, and conceal himself from all ideas and forms, and then it is in the stillness, in the silence, that the Word of God is to be heard. It is to be heard there as it is—in that unself-consciousness. For truth is at the core of the soul and not outside us.

"Therefore, if you would find God, you must empty yourselves. For when one is aware of nothing, the Word is imparted to him and clearly revealed.

"Is the task too great? Do you say to yourselves that you are not good enough to follow this path and that your sins are too enormous," the prior continued as he neared the conclusion of his talk. "I say, He receives you as you are now, not as you were formerly. God bears with years of crime and insult, so that by his divine patience he may conquer man's heart, turn the sinner into a saint, and transform the lover of ease into a model of discipline and penance. In this way he draws good out of the evil of sin. Even though one man were guilty of all the sins committed in the world since the time of Adam, if he truly repented for them God would forgive him and love him as much as an innocent person for God much prefers forgiving great sins to little sins. The bigger they are, the gladder he is to forgive them and the quicker.

"When we think on these things they show us that no creature is more respected than another by God. We are all equal and we are all one. So let us be forgiven and set out to do only good and our ways and our deeds will shine brightly. Then we will bring, each of us in our unique way, a little of paradise to our harsh world."

Lillian sat spellbound on the edge of her seat stunned! At last someone had said it right!

The priest was finished. The sisters applauded loudly and vigorously as he stepped from the pulpit. Lillian turned and clasped Candace to her. As if some improbable scene portrayed in a visionary painting had suddenly come to life, Lillian felt a tremendous surge of strength as the doors to a new journey swung open before her.

Willard Holzheiser was fuming. How did this demon get away with it? This priest had just spouted some of the most outrageous examples of heresy he had ever heard. Just look! All these sisters sitting there applauding, in a rapture, enamored as though they had been with a lover, and the Abbess right along with them. And behold these Beguines. Disgusting. They should be burned! This was going to come to a halt if Holzheiser had his say. He stormed out of the auditorium.

Later that day Holzheiser created a scene in the Abbess' office threatening to file a complaint to the inquisition and demanding that Meister Eckhart never be allowed to speak at St. Mary's again. But Holzheiser had far exceeded his authority and Denis of Dembreux quickly put Holzheiser's complaints to rest. The priest was far too popular to touch, and Holzheiser would have to boil in the same stew as all the others who wanted to bring him down.

But Denis was impressed and he did not want to humiliate his young apprentice. He knew that Willard came from a proud line of defenders of the church. The aggression and audacity he had displayed in the Abbess' office indicated he had real promise to make a mark for himself just like his father had done and his grandfather before him and who knew how far back it went. Denis had a backload of cases, and he promoted Holzheiser to the post of Solicitor Inspector to investigate them.

"Your new job will be to investigate cases of suspected heresy personally and when appropriate to make arrests," Denis said. "You'll present the evidence to our office and we will prosecute the offenders."

Holzheiser fumed when Denis first demanded he forget filing a complaint against St. Mary's and Eckhart, but the promotion soothed his feelings. Every increase in Holzheiser's prestige would make it easier to eradicate heresy and help him set the right example for his newly born son, Leon. Like all the males in the Holzheiser lineage, Leon would follow in Willard's footsteps just like Willard was following the directions set by his father and his father before him in fighting to uphold the laws of the church.

"When will we arrest Eckhart?" Holzheiser asked Denis.

"Keep a file on him. He hasn't done enough now to warrant any action. We'll keep track of him and see where this all leads."

"The day will surely come," Holzheiser said, almost insolently.

Denis regarded Holzheiser warily. "Just make sure your reports are accurate," he warned.

From that day forward Holzheiser began to keep a record on Meister Eckhart. He would need it for the day when it came time to properly deal with him. And come it would, no matter how long it took. Of that, Holzheiser had no doubt. Then this priest would learn whose eye was watching who.

Chapter 9
The birth of a heresy hunter

Willard Holzheiser grew up in the Province of Languedoc. His own father, Werner, had served as an advocate for three Popes, Nicholas III, Martin IV, and Honorarius IV. His grandfather Wurtz had served as a witness in several heresy trials, and his great-grandfather Sebastian had participated in the slaughter of the Cathar heretics at Béziers.

Holzheiser's father, Werner, was convinced the prophecies of Revelations would happen in his own lifetime. All the signs were there, the false prophets, the breakdown in morality, licentiousness, lust, and the rejection of Christ the King. The Lord was coming and when He did, He would wipe the heathen and heretics off the face of the earth leaving the righteous to govern.

Werner wanted to be well prepared for the coming and he wanted to prepare his only son. He looked forward to Willard's fourteenth birthday when he would personally initiate him into God's service. All male children in the Holzheiser lineage went through the same rite of passage and Werner talked about it frequently in the months leading up to the event. For Willard it was like waiting for Christmas. At last he would become a man.

Werner planned to conduct the ceremony himself, but then Cardinal Orsini was consecrated Pope, taking the name Nicholas III. Werner had worked for him on several occasions before, and now the new Pope wanted him in Rome to serve as one of his counsels. It was a great honor, but it meant Werner would have to be in Rome on Willard's birthday. Willard was bitterly disappointed.

"Never mind lad," grandfather Wurtz said. "I will perform the ceremony myself."

Werner approved. "Your grandfather knows the stories better than anyone. Even better than me."

"Alright," Willard said reluctantly. "With grandfather in charge it will be almost as good."

"We will be just as proud of you, my son," his father said.

* * *

When the day arrived Willard waited all morning in suspense until his grandfather came for him.

"Come lad!" grandfather Wurtz said, poking his head through the doorway of Willard's study chamber. "The time is here!"

Willard looked up at the rosy face circled by long white hair and a pepper-white beard with accompanying full moustache. He followed his grandfather obediently into the family chapel.

The chapel was simple in construction with a large cross stationed at one end and a small square glass window tainted yellow and blue just behind the cross. The chapel contained four benches in a row in the center of the room spaced about six feet apart before which were placed cushions for kneeling and in front of which stood a pulpit on which an open Bible rested. Willard sat on a bench facing his grandfather who had taken a seat on the bench nearest the pulpit.

"Today marks your formal initiation," Wurtz announced. "Like your father, myself and your great grandfather Sebastian, you, too, have been called to serve. From this date forward you will receive instruction about the conspiracy that surrounds our holy church."

Wurtz went to the pulpit, picked up a silver chalice and a pitcher filled with wine which had been put there for the occasion, poured some of the dark-red liquid into the chalice and brought it to Willard.

"Drink deep my lad!" Wurtz directed. "This is the blood of the Lord."

Willard drank deeply and felt the warm liquid heat his insides and spread up behind his eyes and into his brain. He handed the chalice back to Wurtz and watched with a quickening dizziness while his Grandfather slowly drained the cup.

"We shall start with a chronicle from your own great-grandfather's past. He himself witnessed the events I shall describe and passed them on to me. I passed them onto your father. You will pass them onto your sons. Note the date well, lad. July 22nd in the year 1209 of our Lord."

The story began with Arnaud-Amalric, Pope Innocent III's legate, and the commander of the crusade, sitting in awe atop his horse surveying the thousands of troops poised for the battle against the Cathars in the field below: company upon company of bowmen; platoons of foot soldiers armed with spears and swords; cadres of knights girded in armor decked out with shields and lances astride snorting, bucking horses; troops with battering rams, catapults, and other siege machines. They all waited expectantly for the command to attack. There came Schein, the field commander, riding along the crest of the hill toward Arnaud-Amalric.

"It's a wondrous sight, this crusade, Arnaud-Amalric," Schein yelled above the clamor. "We've got thirty thousand troops at our disposal. See there on our right and left flanks. We'll first start with the siege machines and blast them with rocks and fire. Then we'll attack!" Even as he spoke the machines began to belch down a rain of fire and stone on the Cathars. Schein turned and rode back until he was in position with his officers and then shouted the command to attack. The first charge was fierce and short. Screams, cries, and groans filled the air. When it was over, hacked and mutilated bodies littered the smoky battlefield. Before the Cathars could regroup Schein sent a second wave storming into the carnage, and then a third, and then a fourth. When they were finished there, the troops swarmed into the town, into the cathedral, and then into the caves in the surrounding hills, killing whoever they could find, Cathars, nobles, and even Christians, if they got in the way.

The Christians were tragic, Wurtz admitted. But innocent casualties are the price of war and the cost of conquest. Who didn't understand that would never understand the road to glory and victory. And it was a stunning triumph. Ten, or was it fifteen or twenty thousand men, women and children slaughtered in a bloody maze.

Wurtz looked Willard over carefully and was pleased. The lad who sat before him with a glazed look in his eyes as though he had suddenly had his virtue torn from him convinced Wurtz he was accomplishing his mission.

"You will come to understand why Pope Innocent promoted this bloody crusade, lad, and why your great-grandfather Sebastian participated in it. Then you will be filled with the strength of Samson."

Wurtz got up and went to the pulpit to replenish the chalice and offered it to Willard again, but the boy declined. Wurtz took a swig and then continued.

"These Cathars, you see, they called themselves Christians who believed in the salvation of everyone. Now we know that is impossible, for the evil are condemned to hell. But these Cathars denied the furnaces of hell, except for the hell they called life on earth. And they believed in reincarnation and remonstrated against our Holy Roman Church. Worse, they murdered one of Innocent's favorite legates, Peter of Castelnau. Your father Werner is even today in Rome working for Pope Nicholas as one of his counsels," Wurtz said, digressing to make the papal connection. "How proud we are of him. Aren't you proud my lad?"

"Very proud!" Willard answered, in an adolescent voice that often broke in the middle of a sentence. "I too shall work in the service of the Pope one day."

"You shall for sure," Wurtz replied and took another swig from his chalice, this time unable to suppress the burp that followed. "Imagine what would happen if these Cathars murdered your own father. What would you do? See them creeping up on him in the middle of the night in some desolate place. See them, lad—the scheming cowards—piercing him from behind with a lance? See his agony? See his pain? See his blood flowing from his body? Are you beginning to understand my lad?"

Willard replied that he thought he understood, and his confusion began to change to resolve.

"It was the last straw for the heretics," Wurtz continued. "These Cathars reached right into Innocent's own back yard to murder a legate he loved like a son. They struck at the Pope himself! God's own emissary! 'Let there be retribution!' That's what Innocent taught these Cathars. 'Retribution!'"

Wurtz's face contorted into what looked to Willard like a tightened fist prepared to strike. "That is how my father Sebastian taught me. It is how I taught your father, and now it is you I teach! When you encounter heresy, lad, stamp it out! Otherwise, it will spread like the venom of a viper that will devour even you. At Béziers, Innocent stamped out thousands of them in one day alone. Now that is a fist of iron! That is standing strong in god's name!"

Willard's grandfather grasped him by the shoulders and shook him hard.

"We are soldiers in the name of our Holy Church! Yesterday, me. Today, your father. Tomorrow, you, my lad! The day after, your sons! You, too, shall fight in the legions of the Lord! This day you have become a man!"

Young Willard felt a rush of power. Surely this was the strength of Samson just like his grandfather promised. He took the chalice from his grandfather's hand, and took a deep, long quaff.

Many years later Willard would say he could feel his destiny take possession of him that day. The story of the Cathars became the seed that would nourish his life's work, furnishing him with the inspiration and hardness he needed to deal with heathens and heretics. And when confronted with heresy and its evil, like he had learned from his Grandfather at his rite of passage into manhood, there was only one path for truth to follow: that was to eradicate all heresy and remove it from the face of the earth forever.

Chapter 10
The new Abbess and her assistant

The full metamorphosis of Lillian did not take long. She remained a nun, but a nun faithful to the spirit of the new God about whom Pastor Eckhart spoke. "Separate yourself from all twoness," he said. "Be one on one, one with one, one from one."

Not long after hearing Friar Eckhart speak, Lillian said to Candace, "I am not a person drenched in sin like the priests insist at confession."

Did not her own conscience fill her with remorse whenever she stepped off the path of righteousness, she asked? Had not the goal of her life been always to do only good?

Lillian had her fill of the world portrayed by the priests where every thought that did not conform to their rules was an act of heresy of some kind. That was what loomed like an ever approaching storm threatening the road ahead that led to a different world to which Lillian aspired where good was the only worthy goal. To admit that the sinless were ruled by the sinful—well, it was like Lillian had always thought yet hesitated to fully accept. The words of Jesus that Candace often reminded her of came to mind. "The good man out of the good treasure of his heart produces good, and the evil man out of his evil treasure produces evil; for out of the abundance of the heart his mouth speaks."

"Pastor Eckhart's God is not the God which rules the divine church according to the Pope and Archbishops where avarice and corruption are everywhere and condemnation of the innocent is rampant," Lillian said

Candace was shocked. She had never heard Lillian speak like that before. Had she made a mistake in taking her friend to hear this priest? But Lillian could no longer turn a blind eye toward the excesses of the church.

"You need to forget this nonsense," Candace replied. "I don't know what has come over you. You'd better go back to saying the beads and we'll all do just fine."

Lillian recognized in Candace the same apprehension that had formerly been hers. She reached out and took Candace's hand.

"Do not worry my friend. Nothing bad is going to happen to us."

"Well I hope not," said Candace, sniffling. "If I had known this would happen I would never have taken you to hear him."

"I am grateful, to you," Lillian said. "We will talk about all that has happened. I will make you understand."

"I hope so! This is—. Well, it's just too outlandish, that's all. Just too outlandish."

"At least I know," Lillian said, "that we are bound together in our love for each other. In that way we will always be together, no matter how we may disagree."

"That is all we need to know. Nothing more."

"Better that you were me than me so that I should not have to take this path I must now take," Lillian said almost sadly.

In the months that followed Lillian gave herself over to intense study and discipline and before long stood at the head in all her classes. As she gained confidence her leadership skills began to emerge so that she advanced quickly in the hierarchy of the convent. First she was put in charge of a dormitory, then the scriptorium. And before long she became one of the Abbess' own personal assistants, of which there were five. All the while, the desire to do good in the world occupied more and more of her thoughts. It was the poor she wanted to help more than anyone. Their suffering was great. But how did you help when you were just an inconsequential part of a giant institution that had no room for new ideas? Yet, would it not always be the same? Today it was the Church that dominated. In another time in another place a different kind of institution would prevail and dictate to the people what they should and should not believe. Those who could not accept this rude authority would be the future heretics, just like Lillian was today. The realization struck her like a bolt from the blue.

"A heretic?" Lillian exclaimed half aloud. "Holy, Mother of Mary! Me, a heretic?" For a moment she panicked and her heart began to race. What should she do? Yet truth was truth no matter what you called it, Lillian said to herself, reasserting her resolve to seek out truth no matter what. She began to breathe easier. Why should she feel conflicted for wanting to help the peasants find truth in their lives for it was truth that led to liberation. "Hallelujah! Christ the King!" Let her superiors name it heresy or whatever they wanted to call it. As long as they did not know that she, Lillian, held these radical views she was safe. She became more determined than ever. She would offer the blessings and benefits of knowledge whenever it was possible to the poor or to anyone else who needed it, and whoever did not like it—well, she would have to deal with that if it was ever required.

"We cannot turn our backs when we are called upon to serve!" Lillian insisted.

Candace was deeply moved when Lillian confided her feelings about the poor and the oppressed. She marveled at her friend's transformation, even though it was a change unlike any she would ever have expected. It worried and upset her. It made her protective.

"It won't be long before you'll be so up there you'll never speak to me," Candace joked. "The next time I turn around, you'll be the Abbess herself."

"I think not," Lillian protested.

But the possibility seemed real enough to Candace. It was no secret that Lillian was the brightest prospect for future prominence of all the nuns at the convent, and as the years had passed the Abbess' health had declined steadily. Everyone knew she was not well. Her fevers were bad and getting worse, but the doctors could not find what was making her sick. They had been giving her strong herbs and tonics but nothing seemed to help. Though no one spoke the words, no one denied that the inevitable seemed near. And true to everyone's expectations the Abbess did not recover from her illness.

The choice of who would replace the Abbess immediately became the topic of the day. Would the new Abbess come from outside or from inside the convent?

Candace was certain she had the answer. "It's sure to be you," she said to her friend.

"Why would they choose me? I am much too young."

St. Clare became an Abbess when she was only 22," Candace said. "St. Adelaide of Vilich was only 17. And she also became the abbess right here at St. Mary's when she was only 30 or so. Not so much older than you."

"But I have no experience for such a position, and the other assistants are ahead of me. You watch! They will send us a new abbess from Paris or perhaps even Rome."

But Lillian was wrong. It came as no surprise to anyone at the convent except Lillian herself when two weeks after the Abbess' death she was chosen to replace her. She was only 23 years of age and the youngest nun ever to be appointed to the position of abbess at the Convent of St. Mary's in Cologne.

"I was right," Candace said, dancing around her friend. "Now I have the inside track right to the top. I won't let you forget it!" She laughed in delight.

The new Abbess laughed too. Though she would now hold a position of leadership and responsibility, her friendship with Candace would never lose its innocence.

"You'll have to change quarters."

"I know," Lillian said regretfully, surveying her cell and making the sign of the cross. "Thank you good cell for protecting me all these years."

"Aren't you glad?" Candace asked.

"It's a big job," Lillian replied. "But yes, I am glad. Very glad. May God grant me the wisdom and strength that I need. You'll help me when I need you?"

"You know I am there for you."

* * *

After she had moved into her new quarters and arranged it to her liking, Lillian invited Candace to visit. It took only a moment for Candace to scan the quarters. Noticeable for its simplicity, the medium-sized chamber contained a table with two chairs, a desk on which sat a candelabra, a cabinet with several plants on top, a book-case filled with books and papers, and a large chest and two cabinets for clothing and other items. A curtained window looked out across the convent grounds. A small separate room served as a bedroom. On the wall opposite the desk, Lillian had tacked a small, wooden frame containing a prayer by St. Francis.

"It's not quite the luxury I had imagined proper for an Abbess." Candace said. "And these bare walls—I bet it gets severely cold here in the winter. We must get you some rugs to hang."

"But look at the view," Lillian responded, pulling back the curtains on the window. "Right out over the convent grounds with the city beyond."

Candace noticed a familiar looking little book wedged in between the papers in the bookcase.

"What are you doing with that?" Candace asked. "You said you would get rid of it. Are you insane?"

"I just couldn't throw it out."

"It's the Gospel of Thomas, a banned book."

"Don't worry. No one knows I have it."

Candace shook her head in disbelief. "Well at least hide it. Promise you'll do that?" she asked with resignation.

Lillian promised that she would.

"And try to remember you are an Abbess now!"

Lillian laughed gaily. Her eyes twinkled.

"You will do well," Candace said. "This job is ideal for you."

"It is because of you that I am in this position."

"Nonsense!" Candace said.

"It is true all the same. You are the one who took me to hear Friar Eckhart. Do you know that he is in Paris doing advanced seminars and is scheduled to go on tour visiting all of the convents around including ours? He will be coming here next month to give the sisters instruction. I shall surely get to meet him."

"You've been keeping track of him?"

"I have indeed. They say he'll be made a Prior soon. They even had him give the Easter sermon at St. Jacques in Paris this year though he's just a junior Professor. I wish I could have heard that."

"Perhaps I will meet him too," Candace said, almost as though she were asking a question.

"I thought you didn't care for him."

Candace looked away and refused to answer.

"Never mind," Lillian laughed. "You shall meet him. I shall make certain that you do. And I am also going to need a number one personal assistant. That person will accompany me wherever I go. Guess who it is going to be?"

"Not me?"

"Do you think you are going to escape your responsibility? I shall need lots of help, and you are going to provide it!"

"You truly are my best friend," Candace said happily. "Imagine me, a personal assistant to an Abbess. I would never have dreamed it in a thousand years."

"We are forever united in our friendship," Lillian said, becoming suddenly serious.

"Friends forever," Candace said with equal solemnity.

"May God bless our path."

"Amen! May God bless our path. Forever and ever!"

Chapter 11
The education of Erich

To start Erich off Lillian assigned him to a special Saturday reading and writing class the nuns taught the children in song school. In the evenings he came home dead tired from hauling the heavy mortar and stone at his new job at the cathedral, but he never failed to put in at least two hours of study so that when Saturdays came he was well prepared. God helps those who help themselves he reminded himself, and he wanted to be worthy and show his gratitude to God for the opportunity he had been given.

The children liked having the big burly peasant in their class. They poked fun at him and he returned it. When he had trouble understanding they corrected his mistakes.

After every Saturday's class Lillian met privately with Erich where she tested him on his schooling and taught him about the history and current events of the outside world. There he learned how to spell Buddha and where India was located, the birthplace of Siddhartha Gautama, the Buddha himself.

Sometimes Lillian's tests went deeper.

"I abhor these injustices by the church committed in the name of Jesus," she said on one occasion.

Erich's eyes flew wide open. The look there told Lillian all that she needed to know. She took it a step further.

"They say because they believe in Jesus they are saved and then use that as a license for calling anyone a heretic who is outside their circle."

"You'll not find traces of me in their circle," Erich said. "I want no part of it."

Erich did not know what to make of the sister's outburst. He had never heard words like these before.

Lillian was pleased. Her intuition about Erich had been correct.

It took three years for Erich to learn the essentials of reading and writing, but Lillian continued to coach him. After two more years' schooling he could read and write very well, and his education was on the same level as any other student who had attended and completed school. From that point forward he no longer needed instruction, but he continued to study on his own while borrowing materials from Lillian to read.

Life went well for Erich and Knorr at the cathedral. They worked hard, and they made friends easily. On more than one occasion they found themselves teetering precariously on the boards suspended from the pillars and walls of the cathedral as they learned their craft. But learn their craft they did.

Erich loved to study new words and Lillian kept him well supplied. He liked to try them out on people to help make them a part of his language.

"This is arduous labor," he said one day to his co-worker Brenner during a work break.

"Arduous?" Brenner said, raising his eyebrows. Before the day was out Brenner and the other masons were having a good laugh at Erich's expense.

"Hey Arduous," Lenzdorfer, one of the foreman called. "Bring that bucket over here, will you? If it isn't too much labor for you, that is." Everyone around clapped their hands and roared.

During this period Erich wrote down all the sayings of Meister Eckhart that he could remember.

One windy day Helmut Ridder entered the cathedral site. He was one of the inspectors for the project and had come to examine the archways on the North wall. This was a day Ridder would be glad to see end. It wasn't that he feared heights, but he didn't go up often enough to feel comfortable on the ladders. He had only agreed to do the inspection because his partner, Mezendorf, had an appointment with the Archbishop who wanted a progress report.

"All you have to do is climb the North Wall and check the base of the archways," Mezendorf said. "We can't have them collapsing on us."

"Why can't it wait?" Ridder inquired. "That's your job and I've got plenty of work of my own."

"What's the problem?" Mezendorf asked. "The Archbishop is going to want to know we've done the inspection. I can't tell him it's been done if it hasn't. C'mon now! Just go to the damned cathedral. Check in with the builder Langer when you get there. Then just climb the ladders until you get to the archways and do the inspection to see that they're structurally okay. That's all there is to it."

Ridder complained some more but in the end gave in.

At the cathedral site, Ridder prowled around looking for Langer but could not find him. The North wall dominated the site and was impossible not to see. A system of ladders, platforms, and scaffolds crisscrossed the wall.

With a sigh of resignation Ridder made his way to the wall and began his climb. At the first level platform he stopped a moment to survey the rush of workmen coming and going around him. He was about 20 feet off the ground and so far everything looked good. The scaffold boards extending from platform to platform were secure and at a width of about two and one-half feet offered ample room for the workman to work on and walk across. Ridder nodded his approval and continued his climb to the 2nd level, and then to the 3rd and 4th. He was beginning to gain confidence. Mezendorf was right. There was nothing to it.

Just two or three workmen and a couple of mortar carriers were working the upper wall. A few more levels and Ridder would reach his destination. At the next platform he stopped to make way for one of the workers who descended the ladder from above. It was Erich. He had just placed his foot on the top rung of the ladder dislodging some debris that had accumulated there which drifted down over Ridder in a cloud of gravel and dust.

"Watch it there!" Ridder yelled. He blinked his eyes, brushed his face and chest, dusted off his shoulders, spat, and moved out onto the scaffold board abutting the platform to make room for Erich to pass.

Ridder removed his cap and combed his fingers through his hair while he waited for Erich to climb down. Out on the scaffold the wind slapped at Ridder's tunic. Grimacing, he pulled his cap tightly over his head, but a gust of wind caught it under the bill and blew it away. Instinctively he reached for the cap, but that put him off balance and he began to topple backwards. He tried to stop his fall, but it was too late. Suddenly he was in the air arms flailing wildly. An arm hit the scaffold hard on the way down, and Ridder threw the other arm around it, latching onto the board with both arms. Dangling from the scaffold one hundred feet above the ground, his weight pulled mightily against his hold. He screamed for help and struggled to pull himself back up on the board.

Erich had just reached the middle of the ladder when it happened.

"Holy mother of God!" Erich exclaimed. His heart raced furiously and he was seized with panic. Only one course of action was possible and he had to act. Releasing his hold on the ladder he leaped for the platform deck a good six feet below. His feet hit the platform with a heavy thud, and from there he sprang headfirst out onto the scaffold board grasping for any part of Ridder he could reach. As he lunged forward his body started to skid off the board, but he managed to retain his hold with his left hand. Seizing Ridder's tunic with his right hand, he pulled hard and tugged and yanked until he had dragged him back up on the scaffold.

Ridder lay sprawled half on the scaffold and half over Erich. They looked at each other for a moment in stunned silence.

"Holy Mother Mary!" Ridder exclaimed.

" That was close!" Erich panted.

"Way too damned close!" Ridder said breathlessly.

They pulled each other to their feet. Ridder clutched Erich's forearm, and blurted out his gratitude. He brushed himself off and climbed trembling down the series of ladders that led to the ground where he stayed the rest of the morning.

When Langer heard what had happened he came to Ridder during the lunch break.

"What the hell were you doing up there?" Langer demanded. "Do you think this is some kind of God damned picnic?" But he softened when he noticed the whiteness in Ridder's face, and motioned for him to follow. "Let's talk this over."

Ridder followed Langer meekly into the foreman's tent.

Later, when Erich came down to ground level Langer called him over.

"I heard what happened," Langer said. "Ridder told me what you did. That was a brave deed on your part."

"Lucky I was there," Erich said. He was not being modest, just embarrassed. He wanted to forget the incident as quickly as possible.

"C'mon along with me," Langer said. "I've got something to show you."

Erich followed Langer into the foreman's tent. Langer went to his table and picked up a purse that lay there.

"Everyone is grateful to you," Langer said. "The Ridder family is a healthy supporter of the church. Ridder asked that you have this." Langer handed the purse toward Erich. "You saved his life."

Money? Did he look like he wanted money?

"I would be little more than a servant, Sir, if I took money for a good deed."

Langer was speechless. Here stood a worker who only yesterday had been a peasant and he was turning down a gift of money because it would make him a servant? Who did he suppose he was in this life?

"That is what Meister Eckhart says," added Erich. "And I believe him. I believe he is right."

"Meister Eckhart?"

"None other Sir. He is—that is, he was the prior in Erfurt, and I went to hear him whenever I could. It was he who recommended me for the job here."

"So that's the way it is. He would be mighty proud of you. You showed great courage today."

"I should not have had it if it were not the less of me there today."

"What do you mean by that?" Langer asked. "Is that what Meister Eckhart taught you?"

"He said the less there is of you the more there will be of God. It had to be the less of me that was up there on the ladder for I have no courage of my own. I was terrified when I saw Ridder fall. I was a coward and afraid to do what needed to be done. But then this strength went into me I know not from where it came. Suddenly I

78

was unafraid and I did not become afraid again until after Ridder was safe."

"Extraordinary!" said Langer. "This Meister! You are very fond of him?"

"I know many of his words. I repeat them so that I don't forget. I was saying them to myself as I climbed the walls today."

"You have done a very good turn! Perhaps you will tell me more about this Meister person of yours someday."

"I will indeed," Erich said, trying unsuccessfully to conceal his pride. "I know him well. He is a friend of mine."

* * *

Employment at the cathedral provided undreamed of security for Knorr and Erich. The workers applauded Erich's courage when he rescued Ridder. They liked the former peasant's sense of purpose and though they joked about it, they admired his determination in learning to read and write. It served them well, too, for they would not let his new skills go unused. At first, it was just a notice or some posting that a coworker had found nailed to his door for some reason and couldn't read. During the lunch break they would sidle up to Erich when no one was around and ask him what the notice said, fearful that it might be an eviction order. Then Langer solicited Erich to take roll and make notes at guild meetings for pay. Erich was suddenly earning extra income regularly.

The years passed and Erich and Knorr became vested members of the Masons' Guild. Knorr showed special skills and learned stone cutting. He rose to the position of assistant foreman for the stone cutting crew. After the high choir was completed and dedicated in 1322, Knorr stayed on at the cathedral to work on the construction of the nave. He and Greta raised three children, two girls and a boy.

But for Erich, life took an unexpected turn long before that. After he stopped seeing Lillian for lessons, he would sometimes send her a note and she would do the same. In this way they stayed in touch and on occasion arranged to meet. Sometimes it was for the purpose of borrowing reading materials, at other times just to talk about what was going on in the world. Lillian also sometimes had news to report about Meister Eckhart which she was anxious to share and which Erich was eager to hear. At one of their meetings, Erich confided that he and Kristen had been thinking of opening a scribe shop for copying reading materials.

"It would be a big challenge, and I'm not sure if we could manage it," Erich said.

"Don't be afraid to try."

"We are trying to talk ourselves into it."

"Remember what you told me the Meister said."

"I do remember. Become aware of what is in you and give birth to it."

"Then what are you waiting for?"

Erich was still hesitant and Kristen was also worried. But then one day after months of preparation, they surprised everyone by renting a two story timber frame house with a shop on the ground floor on Bergstrasse. The plan was simple. They would hang a sign outside announcing that scribe work was done inside. During the day Kristin would tend the shop and take orders for letters to write and documents to copy while Erich worked at the cathedral. He would fill the orders at night and on weekends.

The new shop showed signs of success right from the beginning. In just a few short weeks the business was bringing in more work than they could handle.

"We are going to make it!" Kristen exclaimed gleefully. She seized Erich's hands and they danced in a circle. Then Erich danced solo while Kristen clapped her hands and sang a tune as the happy couple fell into each other's arms.

* * *

The time had come for Erich to leave the Masons Guild to become a fully self-employed scribe. But he hated giving Langer the news and kept putting it off. After the Ridder incident, the two had become ever closer friends. Erich had introduced Langer to some of the Meister's teachings and had become almost like a mentor to him.

Kristen urged Erich ahead. "You've got to do it," she said, one morning just as Erich was leaving for work. "We need to make the break now."

"You're right," Erich said. "I promise I'll do it today."

At the end of the shift, Erich went to Langer's tent pulled the flap back, and went in. Langer, who had been studying a drawing of one of the chapels, looked up and grinned when he saw it was Erich. Then he noticed the serious look about him.

"Why the somber face?"

Erich told him the news. Langer put down the sketch and rose slowly. "I shall miss you," he said simply. "It will not be the same without you."

"The cathedral has grown," Erich said. "It's a magnificent achievement. Hundreds of years from now people will pay tribute to the work you have done here. I've been blessed to help build this, and all because of you I can now look back and say I was a part of this history."

"We will stay close," Langer replied.

"That's as certain as the dawn."

"And don't forget. You still have much to tell me about our friend Meister Eckhart."

"That will always be my great privilege."

"Go with God's grace," Langer said.

Erich nodded. "I'll drop in to say good-bye to the men in a few days. Tell them for me, will you?"

"I will," Langer said. "They'll be sorry to hear the news."

The two men embraced quickly, and Erich turned and left Langer's tent. He did not look back as he departed the cathedral grounds.

Chapter 12
The shop master; arrest of the heretics

The new shop master often kept a quote from Meister Eckhart on the tip of his tongue for his regular customers. Sometimes he would invent his own quips from the Meister's words which he liked to impart when he had the chance.

"Put aside your troubles and be at peace," Erich would advise sagely, if a customer confided a problem for which there seemed to be no solution. "Before you know it the answer will be there."

If it didn't work out, the customer would have a laugh at Erich's expense. "Some wizard you are," they'd say. Or they might tap their fingers on Erich's desk and exclaim, "Still waiting, Erich! Still waiting!"

Once not long after Erich and Kristen had opened their shop a good-looking man—a well-dressed burgher—brought Erich a small book. He wanted three copies made. But before he would place the order he insisted that Erich read some of the book to see if he liked it.

"It is like a book of poetry," the man said. "I value it so greatly that I have had it translated from French into German and now I only want someone to copy it who is of like mind and also appreciates it."

"That's strange," Erich thought. "Perhaps he wants to make sure I can read."

"Read here," said the man, pointing to a passage.

Erich read aloud and without hesitation so that the man would know without doubt that he read fluently. "...and therefore she loses her name in the One in whom she is melted and dissolved through Himself and in Himself."

"How do you like that?" asked the man.

"It sounds like a nice bit of religion to me. You are right. It's almost like poetry."

"Fine! Then I shall give you the commission."

Erich told Kristin about the new commission that evening and read to her from the book.

"'Theologians and other clerks. You won't understand this book—however bright your wits—if you do not meet it humbly, and in this way love and faith make you surmount reason. They are the mistresses of reason's house.'"

"It sounds like the same kind of thinking that might come from Meister Eckhart," Kristin said. "He too does not put much faith in some of the clergy. What is the name of this book?"

"The book is called *The Mirror of Simple Annihilated Souls*. The man said it was originally in French. No author is named though. It appears to be anonymous."

"It is a strange title. What could it mean? Haven't I heard of this book someplace before?"

"That is what I think, too, but I don't know from where."

"I'd be careful of this man. Something is odd here."

"We can hardly throw away a commission. If the man wants to pay for three copies for an anonymous book of religious poetry why shouldn't we take it?"

"You may be right. But even so, be careful. It's still mighty strange."

The man came in the following week to pick up the copies. He examined what Erich had done. "You are a real craftsman," he said eagerly. "How did you like the book?"

"My opinion has not changed. I still like it just fine."

"It is as I suspected when I first met you," the man said. "We heard about you from one of your customers. You are one of us. I can see it. I will have more work for you."

Erich puzzled over this mystery. What had the man meant, 'You are one of us?'

"I should have asked him when I had the chance," Erich said that night when he and Kristen talked over the matter.

"If he comes back you are sure to find out. It will be good to know what this is all about. Let us hope it means well."

Within a month the man did appear again, this time with a pamphlet to copy. He greeted Erich warmly, like an old friend.

"Everyone loves your work," he exclaimed with a little more enthusiasm than was appropriate.

"And who is everyone?"

"A group of people who meet together. We discuss spiritual matters. Perhaps you would like to come sometime? I talked to the group about you, and they voted that you should attend our convocation. We only admit members by unanimous vote."

"I might like to see what it is like. It is not like a church service, is it, where the priests read in Latin? My wife and I have found a church to attend, but even so, one day of Latin in the week is plenty for us."

"Not at all. It is unlike anything you have experienced."

"Can I bring my wife?"

"We were hoping you would. That is one of the differences with our group. You will find the women are as welcome as the men."

"If my wife is welcome what harm could there be? I'll see how she feels about it."

"My name is Walter of Cologne," said the man, and shook hands with Erich. "The next meeting will take place tomorrow evening. Come if you have time."

Walter took a quill and a scrap of parchment from Erich's desk, dipped the quill into an ink well and wrote down the address. He blotted the wet ink dry, looked at the writing to see if it was legible, and handed the paper to Erich. "If you can't come I will give you the date of our next meeting after you have finished copying the pamphlet."

The pamphlet Walter wanted Erich to copy was another anonymous text, this time without a title. After Walter left the shop Erich took the pamphlet to his desk and sat down, leafing through the pages, stopping here and there to read. One passage especially caught his attention.

"Do not obey the prelates, only God."

Erich glanced further down the page where he read, "The Pope is the creator of all errors. The Pope and all his bishops are homicides on account of wars. The prelates should have no royal rights. No one is greater than another in the church. We alone live righteously."

Erich slapped the pamphlet closed! God and great blazes almighty! He was expected to copy this? This was nothing but unadulterated heresy! A chill swept over Erich for he recognized that heresy or not, he mostly agreed with the passages he had read. The conversations with Lillian when she denounced the prelates flashed through his mind. He had agreed with her criticisms too. And he had always possessed these unorthodox thoughts that only a sorcerer might have. Was he a heretic? And what about all the outlandish things sister Lillian said. Was she a heretic too?

Erich decided not to mention the new commission to Kristen for her own protection. If heresy was present he did not want her involved and he did not want to be involved himself. One way or the other, he intended to get to the bottom of the matter. He would go to the meeting the following evening to find out more about this pamphlet and who this Walter was. Perhaps he was some sort of cleric or somehow associated with the church who was justified in having the pamphlet copied. In that case, why throw away a valuable commission? Otherwise, Erich planned to turn the offer down.

"If this is not legitimate he'll go his way, and I'll go mine," Erich reasoned. "That will be the end of it."

The meeting took place at 192 Kirchnerstrasse in the old section of town at 5 o'clock. Erich told Kristen about the meeting and assured her he would be able to easily get back home before curfew closed down the streets at dark.

"Be careful," she said. "Keep on the alert."

"I shall," Erich promised. "After tonight we will know much more about our friend Walter of Cologne."

It was autumn and the early evening was cool and brisk. After a journey down several long and narrow streets Erich turned a corner and arrived at Kirchnerstrasse. The neighborhood was mostly abandoned with few people around. He walked along the street until he came to number 192, an old deserted three-storied stone barn. It was unkept and in a state of disrepair.

Erich pushed open a wooden door with trepidation and entered a large room with shuttered windows. It was completely empty and when the door closed behind him, almost pitch black. Ahead he could see light under and around the cracks in a door and could hear the murmur of voices that grew louder as he approached. To the left diagonally in the corner he could barely make out the outline of something dark that seemed to be a stairway leading to the upper floors.

Erich made his way forward cautiously, groping in the dark, and then pushed open the door framed by light. About fifty people were inside, men and women of all ages, sizes and shapes, and two or three children. Some of the people were seated on about 12 rows of benches in the central part of the room, which were separated by a center aisle. Others in the group stood near the walls or leaned against them. The windows were covered with rotting shutters, and Erich noted that the only entrance or exit to the room was the one in which he stood. Light emanating from flickering rush candles cast long shadows across the room, one of which belonged to Walter who stood at the front speaking to the assembly.

"Come in my brother, and welcome to Paradise!" Walter called to Erich. Everyone turned and looked in Erich's direction. The greeting made him even more uncomfortable. He faked a smile and pressed himself against the wall to the right of the entrance. The door closed behind.

Walter continued speaking to the assembly. "Is it justice that persons of a sinful nature are raised to eminence in the church? Ought not both men and women have the right to preach? Does it say anywhere in the gospels that a woman ought not preach?" Voices in the crowd murmured "Here, Here!" and "Amen, brother!"

"Should not we, as spiritual adepts, by virtue of our knowledge put into action what we know to be true?" Walter continued. "Approach, Sister Betty, and speak for us words of wisdom from the heart as you always do." Walter motioned for a woman to come forward who had been standing beside a young girl on the other side of the doorway on Erich's left. Walter stood to the side as the woman, who appeared to be about thirty-five, moved out of the shadows toward Erich, turned left down the center aisle and advanced to the spot which Walter had occupied. She turned to face the assembly and began to speak in a smooth high-pitched voice.

"You know me brothers and sisters, and you know what it is I have to say. Does it not say in the good book that earth was a paradise that was defiled by knowledge from the serpent? From what quarters comes the serpent that defiles the earth today? Is it not the same that formerly was in Rome that now resides in Avignon?"

The candlelight illuminated wisps of smoke from the candles as they drifted past Betty's face. She was a pretty woman with long, curly-blonde hair that fell down her back.

"What is it they try to tell us that we know in our hearts is false? They say that in embraces and kisses there is sin."

At these words many members in the crowd began to move. Several of those who were sitting on the benches now stood.

"But do we not know this is not true?"

A chorus of "yeses" answered in response.

"We know there is no punishment in the delights of paradise. Are we not the sons and daughters of Adam and Eve? Do not balk. Let us return to our real heritage, to the days when Adam and Eve walked freely in Eden."

The assembly now began to sway back and forth. Some in the group clasped hands.

"Join in brother," said a man standing next to Erich on his right. He was about forty and stood beside a woman around the same age. "We were nervous the first time, too. The children will be put to bed soon in the carriage house in back, and then it gets better. Our rituals involve a simple ceremony honoring Jesus and Mary with Jesus dressed in a pure white robe. Then one of our leaders comes before the assembly, and get this—. He discards one item of clothing after the other along his path! It is a thrilling transformation as he invites us to join him in a simple disrobing as a reminder that we are without sin. But we aren't restricted. We also can get a little closer."

"You know what that means," said the women, knowingly. "We have a grand feast. Then we dance and choose partners. We'll help you disrobe, if you like, when the time comes."

"Holy Mother of God!" exclaimed Erich. "I'm getting out of here!"

At that moment a man holding a rush candle sitting on the second row on the right side facing Betty, leaped up, sidled his way

87

toward the center aisle past people who were seated or standing and then ran up the aisle in Erich's direction. He pushed his way through the exit door which slammed behind him. Startled, the assembly froze. They could hear the man's running footsteps in the adjoining room followed by the sound of the street door as it shut with a bang. A short pause followed, and then a loud drumming sound ensued like an enormous wave rolling toward the assembly room. It felt like an earthquake. Instinctively, Erich ran down the side past the rows of people to the front away from the sound. Suddenly soldiers burst into the room brandishing swords. The assembly cowered in terror. A soldier wedged the door open and then snapped to attention as a tall man with long narrow arms carrying a torch emerged through the entrance, ducking his head because of his height. He stopped just inside the room and appraised the assembly before him with a sneer.

"I am Willard Holzheiser, the Inspector Solicitor for Cologne!" he snapped. "You are a mob of moldy Free Spirit Beghards and under arrest for heresy against the Holy Mother Church. Move to the center and form a column of twos!"

Erich looked around desperately, but saw no means of escape. One by one, in pairs and in small groups, the people moved toward the center aisle talking and whispering in fearful tones. Panic seized Erich. Why had he come here? Why had he not stayed at home snug and safe in his bungalow with Kristen? Who would believe him when he said he was not one of them? Free Spirits! Beghards, the inspector had called them. That group of heretic beggars who held their own religious services without the blessings of the church and claimed their union with God put them above the laws of the church. They were reputed to engage in all kinds of lascivious acts. Of course! Why had he not seen it? That's what Walter was! A Beghard! Now it was too late. Erich lingered back, but it was to no avail. There was no escape. He reluctantly moved to the center aisle where Holzheiser had charged two soldiers to stand at the entranceway and herd the assembly into a column of pairs.

Holzheiser motioned the remaining soldiers to go with him. They left the assembly room and followed him into the dark interior of the adjoining room. There in the center of the room he commanded two of the soldiers to remain to make a head count of the prisoners as they emerged from the assembly room. The two soldiers produced rushlights which Holzheiser lit with his torch. He then marched the remaining soldiers out to the street to stand by for when the prisoners emerged from the building to keep them in line and make certain no one escaped.

While he waited Holzheiser returned to his favorite dream. These sodden little Beghards were fine to round up now and then, but over the years the one big heretic he really wanted remained at large and unrepentant. To Holzheiser, he had become an obsession. How he longed to nail Eckhart to his cross, this so-called Meister, as they called him now. There was one big heretic just waiting to be taken down. When he fell the sound would reverberate through all Christendom! For years Holzheiser had been planting seeds of doubt about the Meister and keeping a well-documented file on him wherever he went, all to no purpose, it seemed. The church's hand was just too weak. If Pope Boniface did not cower so before the throne of Philip the church could have its say and it might not be so difficult to fell a piece of lumber like Meister Eckhart. When would a Pope come along who had the courage to put forward the real agenda of the church and not back down every time some royal authority flexed a little muscle? Eckhart von Hochheim! He was just too strong, too much influence, they always said whenever Holzheiser brought up the name. Damnation and hell together!

Holzheiser, kicked the dirt with the toe of his boot, dislodging a small chunk of earth that skittered aimlessly ahead. At least with Denis of Dembreux set to retire and Holzheiser certain to replace him as the Inquisitor General, Holzheiser's hand would be strengthened. He folded his arms behind his back, and began to pace impatiently back and forth. It was unfortunate his son Leon had been unavailable to come on the capture. Holzheiser wanted to show him how it was done first hand. Already a captain in the papal troops, Leon was following in his father's footsteps and this event would have bolstered his credentials.

Erich found himself last on line alongside a young girl of about nine or ten years-of-age who had paired with him on his left. She was the girl he had seen standing in the shadows beside Betty. Betty was just ahead three or four pairs in line and turned to get back to the girl, but despite her pleas, the soldiers blocked her way and rudely prodded her forward with their swords.

The column began to move into the adjoining room. That room flickered now with the light from the rushlights held by the two soldiers who counted the moving column of prisoners that passed between them. The soldiers stood about half way into the interior of the room. Beyond them, the street door had been wedged open and Erich could see Holzheiser pacing back and forth while some of the soldiers lounged about. It was not yet dark outside.

Once the column was formed and underway, the two soldiers in the assembly room joined the two soldiers in the adjoining room and stayed there to assist them with the head count. Now no soldiers remained in the room, but it offered no place to hide. The candles were burning low and the light was dim. Erich and the girl were approaching the doorway and would soon be in the adjoining room. The stairway that Erich had noticed on first entering the barn suddenly burst into his memory.

Erich saw terror in the girl's eyes. He could also see that intelligence resided there. Good! Any stupidity would destroy what small chance they had. "Do exactly as I do," he whispered. The girl shook her head indicating she understood. Erich held back a little from the pair ahead of them, a man and a woman. The girl followed his lead.

Erich and the girl had entered the adjoining room. Before them stood the four soldiers, two on each side with one of each pair holding a flickering rushlight. They were making certain their count of the Beghards slowly shuffling between them toward the street exit was accurate. Holzheiser did not tolerate mistakes lightly. The soldiers seemed not to be looking in Erich's direction.

"Now!" Erich mouthed silently to the girl with a slight hiss. He dipped low to the floor, and scooted off to the right creeping along the side of the dark room next to the wall in a crouched position. The girl followed in a like manner. The man in front of the pair looked around startled and caught a fleeting glimpse of them but said nothing. Looking back Erich saw the faces of the soldiers illumined by the glowing rushlights and the silhouette of the moving column of figures. The girl was stooped low and following close behind. One of the soldiers was looking in their direction.

Erich found the stairway and scampered as quietly as possible up the steps. The girl did the same. Their hearts were beating madly. They reached the second floor and remained there on the landing out of breath, trying to stifle the sound of their breathing, waiting and listening to see if they had been detected. They heard nothing. Silently, they crept up the remaining stairs to the third floor and entered a large, vacant room.

An open window looked out from the side of the building on the third floor. It was quickly growing dark. Erich peered cautiously from the window toward the narrow street below. Holzheiser stood there barking out orders. As the prisoners emerged from the building, soldiers on both sides moved them down the street to make room for those behind them. Two or three pedestrians stopped and looked on curiously. Betty appeared and then Walter. Behind them followed the forty year-old couple who had stood next to Erich in the assembly room. Finally, the last of the prisoners emerged onto the street, including the children, and a group of soldiers closed in behind them. Holzheiser ordered the column of prisoners and soldiers into a forward march. They trudged around a corner and disappeared from view.

Erich and the girl remained silent for a long time listening closely even after the sounds of the commotion had faded away.

"I think it is safe," whispered Erich. They crept stealthily down the stairs to the adjoining room which now was pitch black. The assembly room was also dark. The candles there had all burned down. The two felt their way along the wall with their hands until they reached the entrance door. It was unlocked. They stepped out of the building and moved down the street. A few people were still about, but no one noticed them. When they reached the corner and made a left turn, Erich began to feel a little more secure.

"Walk normally," Erich said, taking a deep breath. The girl glanced at Erich uneasily and quickly lowered her eyes.

"What is a young girl like you doing at a meeting like this?" Erich asked softly. He appraised her casually trying not to frighten her more than she already was.

"My mother is Betty," the girl said in a small girlish voice. "I have no father." A look of terror remained in her eyes.

"I don't want to frighten you, but I cannot take you to your home. The authorities will seek you out there and force you to renounce."

"But I am just a maiden."

"It matters not to them, my child. After you renounce they will send you to a monastery with the strictest discipline. It will be like a prison. Who was the man who ran out to the soldiers?"

"That was Jay, the husband of one of the women. He betrayed us."

"So that is what happened," answered Erich. He pondered a moment and then made his decision.

"I am Erich. What is your name?"

"Sarah."

"Sarah, you will stay with my wife and me until we can figure out what to do."

"That is too kind of you. She will not mind?"

"No! She is a good woman. She does what she knows is right. It is late. I don't know if we can make it to our home before curfew."

The streets were already hushed and darkness descended quickly as cathedral bells tolled the curfew. Only light from the moon and a few early stars along with the glow from lamps and fireplaces that emanated from shuttered windows dimly lit the way. Occasionally, a pedestrian passed carrying a torch. It was after 8 o'clock by the time Erich and Sarah entered Bergstrasse where they ran straight into the night watchman.

"Out rather late with the daughter aren't you," the watchman stated bluntly, swinging his lantern which shone in the darkness. But it was the beginning of the watchman's shift and he was in good humor.

"We're just down the street. Another moment or two and we're home, watchman," explained Erich.

"All right then. Be off with you. Hurry though. Don't forget to curfew your fireplace and have you a merry night."

"We'll cover it. And a merry night to you, too, watchman."

In another minute they were at the shop door below the sign of a hand holding a quill. In the distance they heard the watchman calling: "All's well! All's well!"

"Quick now! In we go," said Erich. Relief spread across Sarah's face.

As they entered into the cozy shop, Kristen descended the stairs in the rear.

"Where have you been?" Kristen exclaimed with a mixture of anxiety and gratitude. "It's after curfew! I thought you'd never make it!" Then she saw the girl.

"We've got a visitor," Erich explained. He introduced Sarah and described in a few words what had happened. The girl listened stoically as Erich recounted their adventures.

"My goodness! Thank God you made it through! What a nightmare!" Kristen sat down at the desk in the center of the room and drummed her fingers absently on a piece of parchment lying on the desktop there. "That's a terrible thing to put children through."

Kristen did not know yet that Sarah's mother was Betty. Erich put his finger to his lips to warn Kristen. It was the wrong time to talk about Sarah's mother.

"Never you mind my darling," said Kristen. "No one is going to harm you. How old are you?"

"Nine," Sarah said in a disconsolate voice. "Almost ten."

Kristen served Erich and Sarah some rice pudding and then led Sarah up the stairs to their bower.

"You'll sleep in our bower tonight," she said, removing a spare mat and blankets from a storage chest. "And every night after until you feel safe."

Sarah looked questioningly at Erich.

"She's got it right, and she's the wife," said Erich. "We'll see what we can find out about your mother tomorrow. Don't you worry. Whatever happens you'll have a home. And if need be you'll make your home here and we'll be glad for the privilege."

It was a long time before Sarah fell asleep that night. Covered snuggly on her mat in Erich and Kristen's comfortable bower, she lay on her side staring at the blank wall before her with eyes wide open.

"Be brave in this life," her mother had often said to her. "If they ever come for me, be your own person. Do not believe what they say about me. When they tell you your body is a sin know that they lie. It is a gift from God. You will know what I mean in a few years."

Sarah was alone and wanting her mother to be with her. Already so young, and what few illusions fell to her had been snatched away in an instant. She knew what would happen from the stories her friend Jeanine told. Her father had taken her to the execution plaza and made her watch the burnings and the drownings. "It's what will happen to you if you grow up to do sinful things," he counseled Jeanine. "Let this be a lesson for you."

Sarah wanted to cry as the images came to her now that Jeanine described, but no tears came. Her mother would soon be no more and Sarah could not bear what would happen. How could she be brave? But she must just as her mother must. Sarah let her mother's words repeat themselves over and over like a litany at which she grasped desperately to bring herself out of despair. "Be brave, my child. Be brave." The past was gone. Even Jeanine would be gone. Sarah would have to go into hiding. She would never again play with Jeanine and their voices would never again ring together with childhood laughter, good cheer and joy. Now Sarah must be brave like her mother had taught. She must be her own person like her mother said. It was the only choice open.

A voice almost like her mother's hovered over Sarah as she drifted toward sleep. "Life is here to greet you, my child. You are not evil like they would tell you. You are good like your mother said, and God has blessed you."

Tears moistened Sarah's eyes for the first time as the peacefulness of sleep fell around her.

Chapter 13
Erich and Meister Eckhart meet again

Meister Eckhart turned into Bergstrasse on his way to the university more because he was lost in thought than as a matter of choice. It was springtime and the day was brisk and cool. The narrow street with its gentle dips and turns and clean gutter which ran down the middle, the two and three story houses with timber frameworks and neatly lined stores, and the artfully painted signs that hung outside the shops caught his attention and ended his reveries. The Meister had not been in Cologne long and the street intrigued him. Because of the pages, clerks and—judging from their black robes—lawyers he noticed on the street, he concluded most of the shops must have some judicial purpose. The Meister cut diagonally across the street and looked up to see one sign that especially caught his eye. Shield shaped and bright orange, it showed a hand in green holding a feathered quill. Meister Eckhart continued on his way.

Like most of the shops in Cologne, Erich and Kristen's opened directly onto the street. From his desk Erich could look out to see neighbors and other shopkeepers move up and down the street as well as customers and various passersby. Now as he looked a figure crossed the street toward his shop, glanced upward and then moved out of view.

"My Lord! It's Meister Eckhart!" Erich yelled. He leaped from his desk and ran to the door and out of the shop onto the street.

Meister Eckhart had proceeded only a few feet beyond the shop when he heard his name being called. "Can it be?" he exclaimed as he turned toward the voice. "It's Erich of Gotha!"

After they had exchanged a warm and robust greeting, Erich invited the Meister into the small shop with the orange and green shield.

"Do you have a moment?" Erich asked once they were inside.

"I'm on my way to give a class, and I'm almost late," the Meister said warmly. "But for this the class can wait a few minutes. It is wonderful to see you."

Looking around, the Meister took in the neat shelves stacked with parchment and paper of various sizes, some of it blank and some filled with writing. A large high top desk facing the street in which were imbedded several ink wells and a container of fine sand occupied the center of the room. A small stove was visible beneath, which Erich used for drying his writing. Three framed drawings hung on the wall directly to the right of the desk. One appeared to be a likeness of Erich, another of a woman, and the third of a young girl. A bench was placed along the wall under the drawings upon which a white cat snoozed. On the opposite wall hung a landscape painting, and in the rear of the shop behind the desk hung a book shelf suspended on the wall. It contained several books that were for sale. A stairway was visible on the right side of the bookcase.

"I was sure we would meet again," Erich said with delight.

"And so we have," said the Meister.

"You have been in many places. Lillian kept me up to date on you."

"I stayed in Paris for a couple of years after I left Erfurt, the Meister explained. "And after that I was in Strasbourg teaching. Sister Lillian also kept me up on you when she lived here in Cologne. It seems ages, Erich, since we last spoke in Erfurt."

"It must be a good twelve or thirteen years."

"Have you been back at all?"

"Not since Kristen—that's my wife. Not since we moved to Cologne. It was our last trip."

"I just arrived in Cologne a few months ago," the Meister added. "I'm teaching at the university. It has taken longer than I thought to get adjusted here. I want you to know I had planned on looking you up before the year was out. I had hoped Lillian would be around to help get acquainted with everything, but as you must know she has taken the position of Abbess at St. Clare's Convent in Paris. I haven't heard from her recently."

"We hoped she wouldn't take the job," Erich said.

"They want her there to help resolve the uproar going on between the Faculty of Arts and the Faculty of Theology at the university. Have you heard about it?"

Erich nodded. "She said it was about oaths and the right to administer them."

"That's right," the Meister said. "They know she is progressive and were certain she would contribute to the debate. So they practically insisted she take the job at St. Clare's. It's more of an administrative post and gives her time to work on the oaths."

"We hated to see her go," Erich said."

"She told me all about you before she moved," the Meister chuckled. "She wrote that you read and write like a scholar and speak like a sage."

"A sage? Not me," Erich said, blushing. "It is all I can do to get through each day."

Erich described his days as a laborer at the cathedral and how difficult it had been to learn reading and writing.

"Thanks to you and Lillian I can now read and write almost like a Professor," Erich said proudly.

"You have accomplished much. Lillian wrote that you had opened a shop, but I had no idea you had done anything like this! She said you had even found a church to attend that is to your liking."

"We tried several parishes," Erich said. "The best one is not far from here. That's where we go. The priest often quotes scripture in his homilies and urges us to follow the example of Jesus. That's the path to salvation, not empty words, he says."

"The Holy Spirit proceeds only from the Son. Like it says in the scriptures, 'Because ye are sons, God hath sent forth the spirit of his Son into your hearts.'"

The white cat lying on the bench under the three framed portraits looked up, stretched, and yawned. At the same time a medium-sized, golden dog came slowly out from under the bench wagging its tail. The dog walked up to Meister Eckhart, sniffed at him, and waited to be petted.

"What a nice dog this is," the Meister said, patting the dog on the head. "Well there good fellow," he said to the dog. The dog barked and wagged his tail and began to jump up and down, prancing in a circle.

"What is his name," the Meister asked.

"We call him 'Goldie Boy,' Erich said with affection. He went to the dog and patted him on both sides to calm him down.

"He loves blueberry jam. The cat is Cloudy. We named her for the clouds floating in the sky."

Goldie Boy returned to his place under the bench and flopped down there wagging his tail. The Meister walked over to Cloudy, who had glided up landing softly on Eric's copying desk, and began to stroke the top of her head. She rolled over on her back with her paws up and began to purr, signaling Meister Eckhart to rub her tummy.

Erich excused himself and hurried to the stairway where he called up to his wife.

"Kristen, come down! Bring Liese! We have a guest!"

"No creature is more respected than another by God, isn't that right good girl?" the Meister said to Cloudy as he complied with her request for a tummy rub. "He gives to everything alike. And that means you too, little cat."

Kristen did not answer immediately, so Erich called again. "Come down! There is someone to meet!"

"Who is it?" Kristen called back.

"Come down and see!"

Kristen descended the stairs wiping her hands with a towel. A girl of fifteen followed. Kristen was a little shorter than Erich with solid cheek bones and the same country sturdiness. The girl was delicate and taller, slender with long, curly-blonde hair.

"Kristen, it is the Meister," Erich said. "Meister Eckhart."

"My goodness," exclaimed Kristen, taking the Meister's hand. "It is a great honor. This is our daughter Liese. Erich has told me everything. He is always talking about you, isn't he Liese?"

Liese shyly shook Meister Eckhart's hand. This was, of course, Sarah, Betty's daughter.

"Mom is right! Dad is always talking about you and telling us things you've said."

"Would you like something to eat or drink?" Kristen asked, turning to the Meister.

Meister Eckhart did not have time for refreshments, but he did take time to tell a little about his teaching at the university. When he had finished he asked Erich how the shop was doing.

"We didn't know if it would work out," Erich exclaimed. "But it has. We are burghers now, and I am a scribe! We even sell a book from time to time! Can you believe it?"

"You have come far."

"Your letters to Friar Horst and the Abbess Lillian were the keys to our new world," Kristen said.

"Has she written since she's in Paris?" the Meister asked.

"We hear about her through Liese," Kristen answered. "She studied with Lillian for five years. Now they write to each other all the time."

"She likes Paris quite well," Liese said reticently. "But she misses Cologne." Liese did not like being the center of attention and offered only the kind of conversation that allowed her to make a quick retreat.

"Cologne is a great city," said the Meister politely, wondering who Liese was. "I feel much at home here."

* * *

When Erich and Kristen first took Sarah in they needed advice and needed it quickly. It was Kristen who suggested they confide in Lillian.

"You say she speaks out against these church authorities. We need guidance here. This is way beyond us. We've got to trust someone."

"All right." Erich agreed. "I will go talk to her. If she can't help I'm sure at least she won't report us."

Erich sent a messenger to Lillian with a note that he needed to see her on an urgent matter. The messenger returned within four hours with a counter note from Lillian setting up a meeting the following afternoon at 2 o'clock.

When Erich arrived at the guest house at St. Mary's the next day he brought Sarah with him. As was customary, a nun steered them up the spiral staircase and through the passageways leading to the Abbess' quarters on the second floor.

A look of puzzlement registered on Lillian's face when she came out to greet Erich and saw the girl standing beside him. She quickly ushered them into her quarters where they could speak in private and invited them to take a seat at her table. She remained standing.

Erich wasn't sure how to get to the heart of the matter. After he had introduced Sarah he made some small talk gradually filling Lillian in.

"Sarah's mother taught her to read and write and she wants to learn more," he began.

Lillian was glad to see Erich, but this enigma of the girl was strange and awkward. How did she suddenly arrive at her doorstep at St. Mary's with Erich and who and where were her parents? Was the child abandoned just as she herself had been long ago? There was more to tell and Lillian listened with growing fascination to the tale that Erich told. When he got to the part where Walter brought him *The Mirror of Simple Annihilated Souls* to copy, she stopped him.

"*The Mirror of Simple Annihilated Souls*! This is the tract of poetry written by Marguerite Porete, the first women ever burned by the inquisition. Did you not know? But of course, no! How could you have known? It happened in Paris in 1310. She was a mystic, a Beguine who wrote in French. Porete believed her personal relationship with God freed her from the laws of the church. It is a crime to possess her work."

Erich was stunned. "Kristen said there was something mysterious about the book," he said. "But banned or not, I must confess it has the ring of truth to it."

"You are not the first to hold that view," Lillian said, voicing her approval. "But go on with your story."

Lillian sat transfixed as Erich described the adventure in the stone barn with Walter and his followers and the ensuing escape with Sarah from Holzheiser and his troops.

"Brave man!" she burst out when Erich had finished. "How proud I am of you!" She flew to the girl and put her arms around her. "Dear child!" she exclaimed.

"We knew you would understand," Erich said.

Excitement danced in Lillian's eyes. This was not a matter Erich would know how to handle. It was time to take charge.

"And so you and Kristen want to take Sarah in."

Erich nodded.

"Let us think for a minute." But hardly had she paused, than Lillian said, "I've got it. Listen! This is what we shall do. You will say that Sarah is a relative from the country. Then you can say you have taken her in after her parents became ill and died. How does that sound? You can say they ate something bad—maybe tainted rye bread. It's been going around, you know. They call the disease you get from it St. Anthony's Fire."

"St. Anthony's Fire! It's a good sounding story to me. What do you think Sarah?"

But Sarah was wide-eyed, confused, and still a child. She longed for her mother and hardly knew what to think or say.

"She will have to change her name," Lillian added. "And one more item. Not a word of this to anyone. Absolutely not one soul! Well. Kristen is in on it of course. And one other exception. I will tell Candace. We have no secrets. But otherwise if we are to succeed in our endeavor no one must know. Certainly I will not tell this to Meister Eckhart. It could only jeopardize his career if something went wrong and he were somehow connected to our scheme."

As soon as she uttered the word scheme Lillian wished she had chosen another word. Sometimes reality needed a little shading to make it palatable. She smiled in Sarah's direction trying to instill some confidence in the plan.

"This will be our secret, Sarah!" Erich said. "We must do just like the Abbess says. And don't you worry!" But even as he spoke he realized he and Kristen would have to be very careful whenever they spoke about Sarah in conversation with people, even close friends. They would not want to arouse suspicion. And he was amazed by Lillian's response. Was she not afraid of the authorities even a little and what they would do if they ever discovered she was helping to harbor a fugitive? If she was she did not show it. If anything, she seemed almost eager to defy them.

It took no persuasion to get Sarah to disguise her identity. The thought of being discovered was terrifying. The image of Holzheiser holding his torch sneering at the members of the assembly and the vision of her mother reaching back for her while the soldiers prodded her forward with their swords was now lodged unforgettably in Sarah's memory.

After a few days of mulling over dozens of choices Sarah selected the name Liese. It was a pretty name and she liked the way it sounded.

It took a few weeks for Liese to become used to her new surroundings and to feel more comfortable around Erich and Kristen. And once Lillian thought the young fugitive was ready, she enrolled her in the school for girls at St. Mary's. There for the next five years Liese studied reading, writing, speaking, logic, geometry, arithmetic, astronomy, and music. Whether as a means of escape from reality or because she had a natural love of learning, Liese waded into her studies with a passion Lillian had never seen in any of the pupils at the school before. She reminded Lillian of herself when she first began to take her studies seriously after hearing Friar Eckhart speak. Liese even added to her studies by reading books that Erich copied. She began to hope to attend a university when she was old enough, but universities were open only to men in Germany. The prospects were not good.

"If the universities will not take me, I shall give myself a university education. I will find out all the books they read, and I will somehow get them."

"You may be certain we will help you," Erich said.

And Lillian helped too. As she had always done with those she wanted to bring close to her, she gave Liese private lessons often positing her personal brand of instruction that did not hesitate to voice some of her favorite irreverent thoughts. At the same time she made an effort to remove as much authority as possible from the relationship and to give Liese a sense of belonging. That meant allowing her to voice her thoughts and feelings freely, whatever they might be.

In the background lived the ever present image of Betty who wasted away in the dungeon. When she was finally sentenced to death four years after they put her there, Lillian learned about the sentence and that it would be carried out the next day, as was the custom, only because one of her connections passed the message on to her.

Liese was already thirteen when the inquisition executed her mother. Erich and Kristen tried to keep her spirits up, but how could anyone voice optimism in the face of that terrible event? And though she tried to conceal it, the tears that often showed in Liese's eyes offered evidence of the struggle that was gnashing at her on the inside.

In the months that followed, Lillian slowly introduced a mixture of impertinence and humor in the conversations with her young protégé as a kind of tonic to try to ease the pain of living in a culture that had turned Liese into a fugitive and had burned her mother alive.

"This blankety-blank church is on a losing course." Lillian said one day in exasperation. And you know what I mean by blankety-blank."

"Is that right?" Liese said. She had learned that if she challenged the Abbess enough she could get her to say something provocative, even outrageous. "You are an Abbess. And you blaspheme?"

Lillian knew the game of enticement Liese was playing, but she continued. It was becoming a game the two loved to play.

"Hmph!" Lillian said, making a face, which caused the young girl to laugh. "How are you ever going to learn anything if I don't tell you?" She wagged her finger at Liese. "You watch. Now the church has all the power. But it will slip away."

"Those are mighty big words," Liese said.

"And you mark them well," Lillian answered. "How long will the ignorant remain ignorant so that they can always be fooled and made fools of? Forever? I don't think so. Truth is the only foundation worthy of a place of worship, and that is what we must strive to bring here! That is the real church and that is my job. Now, how do you like that, little miss smarty?"

"Indeed I do," Liese said, laughing. She ran to the Abbess and threw her arms around her.

But the day came all too quickly, the day Lillian dreaded, when she had to tell Liese she would be moving to Paris.

"I have no choice," Lillian did her best to explain. "Friar James in Paris insists he must have me there to join his side against the swearing of oaths at the university. They want me to take the job of Abbess at the St. Clare Convent. It will be more administrative duties than like being in charge of the nuns here at St. Mary's and will free me up to devote my time to this effort."

"Is it that important that you absolutely must go?" Liese asked, feeling the pain of a future without Lillian's presence.

"It is one of the most important debates of our times."

"Very well, if that's the way it is," Liese said stoically. Fate had taught her how to reconcile quickly with disappointment to soften the blows. "I can only take it to be for the best. But you must explain it to me. This sounds like something I should know about."

"Of course you should," Lillian said. "The question is, should the scholars at the university be forced to swear an oath of allegiance to the universities under threat of excommunication and expulsion from the university? The authorities even want them to swear to turn in their friends or neighbors under threat of prosecution if their friends should ever engage in any kind of rebellious activities."

"That's having your cake and eating it too."

"That's what the Friar also thinks, and I am with him. The university wants to protect its privileges acquired long ago through oaths provided by different monarchs and pontiffs. Even Pope Gregory IX made such an oath. Again, we say "no." We believe we must keep the state and church out of our universities, and vice versa. It all goes to deeper levels of the abuse of power over the individual and by the individual."

"You know where I stand there," Liese said firmly.

"That is why I must go," Lillian said. "The Friar knows that my voice will be respected because I am an Abbess. I will have to be subtle, naturally. These are delicate subjects."

"I understand what you have just said. You should go. It is important work, and it is your duty."

104

"Do not worry, my dear. We shall write to each other all the time. Send me all your thoughts, just like we do here. I will be there for you always."

I will write to you almost every day."

"And I shall write right back just as often," replied Lillian. "Thank you for understanding."

* * *

It was thrilling to meet Meister Eckhart, and Liese could not resist basking for a moment in the presence of the famous man. How many times had her father and mother and Lillian talked about him. Yet the Meister had seemed like some vague abstraction. Now here he stood in the flesh and she was there with him. Liese could not help herself. She felt proud to meet this giant of learning.

"Liese has an excellent schooling," Kristen said.

"When Lillian left for Paris it meant the end of school," Erich added. "But Liese reads all the books and pamphlets I copy. She could go into a university today and take right up."

"How old are you?" the Meister asked.

"Fifteen!" She looked expectantly at the Meister wondering if she should say more.

But the Meister had already made his plan. He liked the young girl. She was shy, and compassion and intellect shone in her eyes.

"That is old enough. Perhaps you would like to attend some of my classes as my guest? They do not admit the ladies, but I am personally inviting you. You may come also," he said to Kristen. "And of course you must come too, Erich, if you like."

"Someone should remain here at the shop," Kristen answered. "We don't dare close." Kristen was glad for the excuse. She hated the idea of sitting in a class.

"You can be sure that I'll not miss it," said Erich.

"I would love to come," Liese seconded.

"I hold my lecture class Fridays at 1 o'clock," the Meister said, rising to leave. "That is the class that would interest you most. Come this Friday if you like. We will be discussing how God is free of everything and therefore is everything. It is a topic that will make us think. Now then. It has been wonderful talking with you. But now I am going to be very late for my class. I really must go."

As soon as the Meister had departed Erich sat down with Liese for a talk. It was his duty to be concerned about her safety and he did not want her to take unnecessary risks. But he also needed to help her achieve her goals.

"Do you think it is wise for you to attend the Meister's class?" Erich asked tentatively. He watched Liese's eyes for a reaction.

"The danger is long past," Liese answered. "I must live like a normal person. How shall I live if I let fear prevent me from doing what I should do?"

"We must think about the Meister too," Erich said.

"If he is the man you say he is, he could only be on my side if he knew about me," Liese answered.

Erich nodded, startled by how outspoken the girl sometimes was. Many times he had warned her to be cautious, but he still worried that she might someday say the wrong thing to the wrong person.

"Alright!" he said. "It is settled. And I agree with you. I just wanted to talk it over. When the time comes I will tell the Meister your story. That way nothing will be hidden between us. If he objects he will tell me."

"What about Lillian?"

"I will write her that I intend to tell the Meister your story and that it can't be avoided. I'll put it in a way that I know she will agree."

"Isn't it a fantastic opportunity?" Liese exclaimed excitedly. "I shall be attending a class at a university with one of the greatest teachers in Europe. I am so glad you are here," she said suddenly, her voice filled with emotion. "If you hadn't come to the meeting that terrible night so long ago where would I be?"

"That goes for us too my child. Kristen and I, we are the fortunate ones. I think God has blessed us all."

"May He keep us safely with His grace," Liese said. She went to her father and hugged him warmly. "Thank you dear dad. Thank you, thank you, and thank you a million times."

Chapter 14
Classes with the Meister

The overworked and disgruntled provost complained to the head about the young woman attending Meister Eckhart's class.

"He can't give her permission!" the provost insisted. "She's not even registered. And her father is attending too. It's a disgrace. What is this, family night at the joust?"

The head dismissed the provost's complaints. What the Meister wanted the Meister got. It was that simple. He was far too important.

"Important my ass," said the provost. "It's never been done before at this university. I won't stand for it." But the head's authority far outstripped his. He stood firm.

"Pretty soon he'll have nothing but ladies attending his classes," the provost huffed. But he gave in. It did not pay to fight with the head.

Liese listened carefully to the Meister's lectures. After classes she wrote down her thoughts in her diary and shared them in her letters to Lillian.

"You should have heard him," Liese wrote. "First he said if his own mouth speaks and declares God, so too does the being of a stone! How does a stone speak, I ask you? Then he spoke about a light in the soul which is uncreated and uncreatable. He said the light is only satisfied in that most inward place where everyone is a stranger. He said it is immovable but it moves all things and from it *all forms* of life are conceived which, possessing the light of reason, live by themselves. Write quickly and tell me your thoughts on the meaning of these words. I must know what they mean. Mom and Dad say hello. The Meister wanted to know all about you. Love Liese."

"I cannot tell you how pleased I am to learn you are coming under the spell of the Meister," Lillian responded. "You must convey my best wishes to him. I owe him a letter. Besides his profound realizations about God, he is also a scholar and most adept at debating the Christian traditions of the old church masters with the other prelates. They sometimes go around and around arguing the most abstract kind of stuff. That may not please someone opposed to the church. But you will find that the Meister lays out a path leading to the direct experience of God. And he has much to offer that clarifies the message that Jesus brought to our world. These are the areas where he is most helpful to us. Can you imagine saying the kinds of things he says in our times? What audacity! You ask about the meaning of his words. Surely they mean that God is in the innermost part of everything. Even the sun and the planets that turn around our earth, even the bees and the tiniest of ants. God is not reserved just for we human beings. No. He is everywhere. Even a stone possesses His being. It is the same when the disciple Thomas wrote that Jesus said, 'split a piece of wood, and I am there; lift up the stone and you will find me.' It is the voice in the stone, the voice in a piece of wood, the voice of Jesus, the voice of Meister Eckhart, the voice of you, and the voice of me. It is the voice of God. We who are not God all declare God in the way that is given to us and in that way we share with God. Now don't you tell anyone I mentioned the Gospel of Thomas. There are some here in Paris who would throw a fit to know that their Abbess is familiar with this man's work. Love to all. Until we meet again. Affectionately, Lillian."

"She is such a heretic," Liese laughed as she read Lillian's letter.

When Erich visited the Meister's classes he would take notes on a wax tablet which he inscribed with a bronze stylus. Then he would copy his notes onto parchment when he had time. Once he showed his notes to the Meister. They were neat and clearly stated with a hand that was steady and easy to read. The Meister was impressed.

"Attending the Meister's class is like going to the cathedral in Erfurt again," Erich said to Kristen and Sarah. "Except there is no cathedral."

"You have to find all that great choir of beauty on the inside now," chided Kristen.

"Not, so very easy," Erich lamented.

"A lot of junk in there, ornaments and things for which people have little use if you ask me," Liese said playfully.

108

The months flew by and Erich and Liese kept attending the Meister's classes. They would sometimes wait to speak with him alone after class if it appeared he had time. Each recognized the other's need to be alone with the Meister so that sometimes just Liese would wait and at other times Erich.

Liese sought advice about her future. She hoped to marry, but she did not want to be a housewife. How might she carve out a career for herself in a world that did not want educated women? One alternative was to become a scribe like Erich. Or she might become a writer. These were the kinds of matters she discussed with the Meister.

"You must investigate Italy," the Meister said. "They are more open-minded there about education than in Germany or France. I have heard the University at Salerno will take exceptional woman, even to study medicine. You have been coming to my classes for over a year now and I know you are exceptional. If you ever want a recommendation you only need to ask."

Liese wrote to Lillian and relayed the Meister's words.

"This is an excellent idea," Lillian wrote in her next letter. "We must learn more about the University in Salerno and begin making plans for how we shall get you there. All is well here in Paris. You should come here just to see the Archbishop, how he goes about with his nose in the air ranting on about his sacred rites. Everyone kisses you know where whenever he is near."

Liese knew she was fortunate to have a mother and father like Kristen and Erich and a friend like Lillian and Candace too. Mostly the young girl stayed by herself and made no effort to cultivate friendships. She was a fugitive who was forced to keep her past to herself. It was too complicated to reveal even the most mundane facts about her background to anyone, and whenever she tried she found herself caught in a swarm of lies she had to tell to protect herself. She hated lying. And so she mostly withdrew whenever she found herself in the company of others.

Thanks to Lillian's coaching, Liese learned how to think for herself and meditated over serious subjects like what was sacred and what was not. Sanctity? That came from within. Rituals? They came from without. What was holy or not depended upon the sanctity of the individual, not the rituals. That was how Liese viewed it. And it was the same that the Meister taught. If the church wanted to celebrate true sanctity that was fine. She believed in sanctity and holiness. But it had to be real.

Liese loved her friend Lillian. Sometimes it was hard to believe she was really an Abbess. One day she had even spoken out against the Pope. And she believed that women had the same rights for education as men. That was dangerous thinking. Now here stood Liese following in her mentor's footsteps. And then there was the Meister. What was Liese doing at a university attending Meister Eckhart's classes anyway? It was unheard of in Germany. Bad enough that young girls were sometimes allowed to attend secondary school. Why wasn't she married and at home taking care of children and looking after a husband? Moreover, with the kinds of thoughts Liese harbored it seemed that she, too, was tainted with heresy all right, and she was glad for it. Glad! When Betty was burned any illusions Liese still held about the church were shattered forever. What kind of church would destroy her mother and brand her a fugitive? To accept or reject the church and its rituals was a question of the times. It led down many paths. It had led Betty to destruction, and now Liese had to ponder where the path she envisioned might lead.

Of course, Betty had been burned as a tramp who practiced free love. Liese did not even know who her own father was. How would anyone expect the daughter of a whore like that to view sanctity, rituals, heresy? Yes, this was the way people thought, Liese said to herself, all too aware of the times in which she lived. To them, her mother was a whore. It was sad, and the memory of Betty still hurt badly.

Whenever thoughts and memories like these passed through Liese's mind she had to pause for a moment to reflect on the bitter irony that had put her in a position where she could speculate freely about such matters in what had developed into an uncompromising search for truth. It was a truth that liberated, and it provided wings for the spirit's flight.

In his private meetings with the Meister, Erich sought always more knowledge and greater insights. The interactions between the Meister and Erich had forged a bond of understanding between them. Added to that, they had grown up in the same surroundings, walked the same fields, visited the same towns, talked with the same people, even looked up to see the same clouds, skies and stars above. The Meister looked forward to his conversations with this former peasant from Gotha. It was immensely rewarding to witness the change that had transformed Erich from an illiterate peasant into an articulate individual who expressed his concerns about life and the world in meaningful, thoughtful words.

"Some of my most advanced students should know what you understand already," Meister Eckhart said to Erich one day.

Erich had been waiting for an opportunity to tell the Meister about Liese's past, and it seemed like the time might be right.

"I would like to tell you about Liese," he began.

"I will be pleased to hear about her," the Meister said.

"She came to us as a fugitive six years ago," Erich said, pausing to wait for the response that would tell how much more of Liese's story the Meister might want to hear.

"I am glad to hear she has made it through safely all these years," the Meister responded. "Many of those sought by the authorities do not find a safe haven."

It was the kind of response Erich had hoped for. Now he had no hesitation in telling the Meister the story of Walter and Betty and how they had sought to relive the innocence of the Garden of Eden. He told how the soldiers and Holzheiser rushed in and how he and Liese narrowly escaped.

"That is an extraordinary experience!" exclaimed the Meister. "You have been given to perform heroic deeds to rescue the innocent. This is a special talent. It is a gift from God!"

"We kept Liese here with us to live after that. She was glad for it, as were we. Lillian helped. It's hard to believe, but Liese is fifteen already. The inquisitors tortured Walter and Betty to make them turn over the names of more Beghards," Erich continued, "but they would not do it. They burned them in 1322."

"I heard about it. A terrible event. It happened while I was still in Strasbourg. I could not have imagined you were connected in any way."

Erich told the Meister how he had gone to the execution plaza and followed the cart along that carried Betty from the prison to the plaza on the day she was burned. He wore a scarf that belonged to Sarah and got right up next to the cart so that Betty could not fail to see it. In this way he communicated that Sarah was safe.

It had been four dismal years since Betty's capture, years of torture and despair where hope seldom penetrated the gloom of the dark dungeon room where they had thrown her with the cockroaches, spiders, and rats and mice, but when Betty saw the scarf she recognized Erich from the assembly meeting, and gladness filled her heart.

"I see that my daughter is in good hands," she cried out. "Send her my eternal love and tell her she must be brave and never lose faith in God or Jesus no matter what anyone says! Tell her to listen to that still, silent voice within. Tell her to love everyone, even her enemies."

Some surrounding the cart turned toward Erich, and one brawny man over six feet tall stepped threateningly in his path. Erich nimbly stepped around him and disappeared into the crowd as the cart rolled on. He turned just in time to see Betty reaching out toward him, her fingers spread apart clutching at nothing, her head turned to the side, her curly-blonde hair scraggly, matted, and dirty, her mouth open, her lips parched and cracked, her eyes filled with the expectation of the fate that awaited only minutes away.

"Liese was deeply hurt and saddened by what happened," Erich said. "She was already thirteen when her mother died, just two years ago, and she still struggles to get over it. All these tragedies. It is the leaders who have it wrong. Not the little people. Not the monks and the friars and the nuns and the brothers and the sisters and the priests and the others who assist and heal and teach goodness and the teachings of Jesus. It is the big ones and those among the little ones who want to be like the big ones. They are the problem."

"You speak eloquently today."

Erich protested.

"No!" insisted the Meister thoughtfully. "There is real eloquence in your words. Take a look around. There are many masters among us who have no religious understanding. They are not able to discern what God is in the least of creatures, not even a fly. But you have understood something. These times are hard on people. They speak to our lower selves and keep us enslaved. We must rise from our bondage toward our true nature. Liese has an excellent start and you are helping her along the way. I am glad to know her story."

Surprised by the Meister's compliment, Erich could not resist adding, "People do not see beyond the limitations of their times to simple truths that are within easy grasp for every era, rich and poor alike, those with power and those with none. All it takes is a compassionate heart."

Except with Kristin and Liese in the shelter of their home, Erich had never expressed his own personal innermost thoughts to anyone before.

The conversation had reached its final cadence.

"I would like to ask you one favor, if I may," Meister Eckhart said. "This Archbishop here in Cologne. There are rumors he wants to begin an inquiry about me. Some complaints concerning my homilies were sent to Venice a year ago. I answered the charges, but now other complaints have surfaced. I can't imagine what they are all about. It appears the Archbishop has been asking questions and may want to make matters difficult."

But when the Meister said he had answered the charges, he had not at all dispelled the complaints of his critics like he thought. They had been keeping an eye on him for years. The trouble for everyone had started when more than one hundred bishops as well as abbots, prelates and other clerics convened at the Council of Bishops at Vienne on the Rhone River in October of 1311. Heinrich von Virneburg, the Archbishop of Cologne, had already targeted Beguine and Beghard households as havens for Free Spirits at the Cologne Synod he had assembled four years earlier. Now the Council of Bishops picked up on the theme and placed it high on their agenda at Vienne. After some intense infighting the Council issued two Bulls. The first declared that some Beguinages where the Beguines lived were good while others engaged in activities contrary to the interests of the church and required supervision. But the second Bull, the one they called Ad Nostrum, accused the Beguines of engaging in unredeemable heretical practices, especially in German lands where men like Virneburg held power. There these Beguines were said to engage in free love under the pretext that they had become unified with God and so lived above the law of the church. After the Council adjourned, the inquisition mounted an unrelenting assault on Beguine and Beghard communities.

It was still a disquieting time two years later when Meister Eckhart arrived in Strasbourg as the new Vicar of Teutonia with orders to oversee the Beguine convents in Southern Germany. Not only was he responsible for the instruction of the Beguine convents, he had to protect them from the assault of fanatic priests still inflamed with the spirit of Vienne. It was inevitable that the Meister developed powerful enemies while he carried out his duties. That the Meister gave his sermons in his native German was bad enough, but some clerics were enraged by his support of the Beguinages.

Among those on hand to take note of Meister Eckhart's activities was Willard Holzheiser. He had participated in the Council's meetings and gone on to Strasbourg where he assembled a dossier on Free Spirit activities.

"Did you hear what this Eckhart says," Holzheiser asked, cornering one of the Bishops at the cathedral in Strasbourg one day. "He claims that all creatures are alike."

"How could I not hear," the bishop replied. "His words are being repeated everywhere."

"Even some of the Dominicans are furious. They're distancing themselves from him. Already they wonder why he is so eager to protect these Free Spirits. The way I see it, the apple falls not far from the tree. He's a little too wise for his own good, this one. He'd better watch his step. The trap is set. It's all I can say."

The Bishop glared at Holzheiser with contempt and walked away. He did not like to be corralled and he did not like people who tried to control others in order to help them succeed with their personal plans.

* * *

"It's nothing to worry about, Erich," The Meister continued. "But if anything should happen to me would you take the notes you have made in my classes and deliver them to my assistants Charles Egmund and Michael Altenbrenner? Michael is also my secretary. You can reach them at the university. They know that if anything ever should go terribly wrong, they are to deliver my work to my colleagues Johannes Tauler and Heinrich Suso."

"Egmund and Altenbrenner. Tauler and Suso. I will remember the names and write them down as soon as I have quill in hand." To himself, Erich said, "Imagine that he deems my notes are that good. He said that I spoke eloquently. Me? Eloquent?"

"Let me be clear so that there can be no mistake, so you will understand beyond all doubt," the Meister said. "There is something I want you to know. We have three kinds of knowledge. The first is sensual, the eyes sees things at a distance. The second is intellectual and is much higher in rank. The third represents that aristocratic agent of the soul, which ranks so high it communes with God, face to face, as he is. It has nothing in common with anything else. It is unconscious of yesterday or the day before, and of tomorrow and the day after. For in eternity there is no yesterday nor any tomorrow, but only Now, as it was a thousand years ago and as it will be a thousand years hence, and is at this moment, and as it will be after death. Do you understand?"

"I think I do," Erich said earnestly. But even as he spoke these words he was not quite sure just how deep his understanding went. It might take years to really understand what the Meister was talking about, and even then would he really understand?

"Good!" the Meister replied. "I could leave you with no finer gift."

"I shall never forget it."

Back home Erich immediately went to his desk and copied down the names Johannes Tauler and Heinrich Suso, Charles Egmund and Michael Altenbrenner so that he would not forget, though he could not imagine he would ever need to use them. Who would want to harm his friend the Meister? Who was this Archbishop, anyway, and why would he stir up trouble?

Chapter 15
The plot

"Gentlemen, Gentlemen! I cannot bring charges against this distinguished Dominican cleric. His popularity and fame are immense. He has come here to fill the very same chair in our university once occupied by Albert the Great."

The words came from none other than the powerful Heinrich von Virneburg, Archbishop of Cologne. Seated at the Archbishop's library table, a tall and thin Willard Holzheiser glanced at his handsome son, Leon, sitting across from him, and took in the words of the Archbishop who remained standing as he spoke. Holzheiser had told Leon the task would not be an easy one. Even so, in Virneburg, they had an ally whose reputation as a warrior against heresy could hardly be surpassed.

Holzheiser had been trying to talk Virneburg into bringing charges against Eckhart ever since the Meister had arrived in Cologne. The priest had been skating on thin ice challenging the church for years with his heretical utterances, Holzheiser insisted. But Virneburg always countered that Eckhart was so skilled with his oratory he could skate full speed right up to the brink of the abyss and stop on a groschen.

In recent months that had begun to change. Some clerics in Cologne had added their voices to bring Meister Eckhart down. They did little to conceal their dislike for this protector of Beguine sects who taught in his native tongue and made no attempt to hide his pantheistic leanings. What a thorn Eckhart must have been in the side of John of Dürbheim, the Bishop of Strasburg, when Eckhart was the Vicar there, they said.

The problem was how to get enough on Meister Eckhart and establish charges that would stick. But Holzheiser had learned from one of his sources that two of these clerics, Hermann of Summo and William of Nideggen, both Dominicans, had presented a list of charges against Eckhart to Von Virneburg himself. Holzheiser had been lobbying for this personal meeting with the Archbishop ever since. Now his persistence was paying off. The invitation to Virneburg's own palace was evidence that the Archbishop was beginning to waver.

"The Dominican order has bestowed this prestigious honor upon Eckhart von Hochheim," Virneburg continued. "He is known everywhere as a great teacher and everyone knows his name. That is why they brought him here to the university."

"That is just the point," countered Leon artfully. "Eckhart is a Dominican. If they had appointed a Franciscan to take Albert's chair we would not have these problems."

"How he has grown," Holzheiser said to himself, taking pride in the positive, unyielding manner in which his son presented himself. Already there were many who regarded Leon as almost his father's equal, which was no small comparison to make considering that after three decades of pursuing renegade heretics, Willard Holzheiser had firmly established a reputation as the most relentless hunter of heretics in Germany. But Leon held an advantage in that his good looks and wining manner made him someone people in positions of power liked to rub shoulders with. Not so with Willard, who, added to his stern appearance, had an arrogant, even abrasive air about him. Leon was not only handsome, he was unencumbered, ruthless, and cunning. It would not be long before his father would be handing the torch to him. With a little luck and the Holzheiser family fortitude, it was anticipated that Leon would eventually gather even more fame as a hunter of heretics than Willard himself.

Virneburg noticed his guests were both sitting stiffly and chuckled to put them at ease. Holzheiser responded with a short smile. He didn't smile often, but when he did, his eyes finished the production by darting left, then right while his lips snapped back to their normal position as though to announce the moment of conviviality that had momentarily escaped had been captured again.

"Gentlemen. How will it look?" Virneburg said, his hands on his hips as he swiveled slightly toward Holzheiser and then back toward Leon. "He has only been here a little over a year and I am to turn around and make accusations against him? Nicholas of Strasbourg, the temporary Vicar-General of the Dominican order here in

Germany, has already made his own charges and then exonerated him. What justification, then, is there for further accusations?"

Holzheiser recognized that the Archbishop was testing him.

"That was a sham," Holzheiser responded bluntly. "Nicholas is a Dominican. The Dominicans knew that trouble was brewing and tried to head it off by creating this fake charge against Eckhart that nobody could win. Why Nicholas is a subordinate of Eckhart, his colleague no doubt. Of course he found him innocent. The Pope sent Nicholas here because he doesn't want to deal with all this and hoped to put the suspicions about Meister Eckhart to rest."

"Excellent!" Virneburg commented. "I had hoped you had informed yourself on the finer points of this case. But even so, new charges will be difficult to bring. Look at his resume. Prior at Erfurt. Prior at Strasbourg. Vicar of Thuringia. Invited personally to Rome by Pope Boniface when he was Pope to defend the papacy against King Philip IV. Master's degree from the College of Paris. Provincial of the Dominicans in Saxony. Vicar of all of Bohemia. Nominated for Superior of the whole German Dominican Province. Professor in Paris. Now he is a Professor at Cologne. And the books." The Archbishop strode to the book shelves in the library and fanned his fingers across a row of books at eye level. *The Book of Divine Comfort. Talks of Instruction. Parisius Habitus, Opus Tripartum. The Book of Wisdom. The Book of Propositions, The Commentary of Genesis,* and on *Exodus,* and on *Ecclesiastes,* not to mention the *Commentary on the Gospel of John.* Then there's the *Prologus in opus propositionum,* the *Prologus in opus expositionum I* and *II,* the *Collatio in libros Sententiarum* and all the other lectures, plus the Sermons. You see! And there is yet more. This is not just some everyday nobody you want me to charge. This is Meister Eckhart himself! What good would it do, anyway, if we were able to successfully censure him?"

"Censure?" responded Leon instantly, almost before Virneburg had finished. "Who is talking about a censure? He is to be brought before the tribunal!"

"What? Are you serious? No theologian of his rank has ever been charged with heresy. Not in the entire history of the church!"

"Shall that excuse a crime?" asked Holzheiser. "He is abusing his position and misleading the common people. Letters were sent just last year to Venice at Dominican headquarters complaining that he says things to the commoners that, and I quote, 'might easily lead his listeners into error.'"

"And how did Eckhart respond?" Leon asked. "Did he take the complaints seriously, or did he escape them with his usual verbal acrobatics."

Holzheiser got up from his chair, went to the end of the table, and withdrew a sheet from a file among a stack of documents he had piled there when he first entered the Archbishop's library.

"This is how Herr Eckhart responds," Holzheiser said, reading from where he stood. 'If the ignorant are not taught, they will never learn and none of them will ever know the art of living and dying. They are taught in the hope of changing them from ignorant to enlightened people.' What is he talking about? Is the church not there for all the people? Do we not offer all the sacraments, christening, baptism, confession, marriage, and the last rights? What more could a peasant want? Do they need these complicated ideas about enlightenment put in their paths like stumbling blocks? Who does this Eckhart think he is? Is he above the Holy Mother Church? It is the church that is enlightened, not Meister Eckhart!"

"I am familiar with these charges. It is a matter I have under advisement. And I am aware that as a result, grumblings are beginning to sound against Eckhart even in the upper echelons of the Dominican order. But this is old stuff. Surely you have not come here just to discuss this. If you want to bring a charge of heresy you must have a legitimate case."

"We need to wipe out this heresy mess that is growing and festering all over Cologne. It is not safe for the children," Holzheiser said defensively, returning to his seat. He brought the stack of papers with him and deposited them with a thump in front of Leon on the table.

"Nor for we Franciscans," Leon added, slapping a hand down on the stack of papers as soon as it hit the table. "Last week we arrested Brother Matthew, one of our own Franciscan brothers. He was disseminating Free Spirit ideas. Where did he get them? It was the same kind of insanity this fool Eckhart of whom you are so proud is spewing out—that there is no devil, and such nonsense."

"I have not said I was proud of him," countered Virneburg, turning sharply toward Leon. "I am merely pointing out the complications of putting someone with the stature of Meister Eckhart on trial. There are many problems here. Especially since he has already been exonerated from charges."

A slow smile began to spread over Virneburg's face. "It would be a just end to an unjust beginning, though," he said slowly but with growing enthusiasm. "Not only would every real upholder of the law be pleased to see this heretic brought down, it would help consolidate Pope John's power as well. Clearly, it would serve as a superb example everywhere."

"Exactly!" exclaimed Leon. "Look at him anyway. Teaching and preaching in German. He thinks he is better than all of us."

"It is time we stamped out this heresy once and for all," Holzheiser added, seizing the moment. "These indiscriminate roundups we make are good, and they keep heresy in check, but they have not accomplished our goal which is to eliminate all enemies of the church."

"You cannot blame me!" snapped Virneburg, bridling. "I have gone after the brothers and sisters of the Free Spirit relentlessly here in Cologne. I have done more than almost anyone to eliminate the Free Spirits in Germany."

"Well spoken," Leon said. "Without leaders like you they'd be fornicating in the streets. But the problem is still with us. These Free Spirits squirm into other organizations and infest them with their promiscuous ideals. Take the Beguines, the Beghards. Formerly, they were in good standing. The Beguines for the women, the Beghards for the men. They did good works, charitable works. Then along come the Free Spirits and suddenly the Beghards are dancing around naked performing all kinds of lewd and lascivious acts."

"It was I who first reported that the Free Spirits were taking refuge within the Beguines and Beghard households," Virneburg responded with irritation. "A long time ago, way back in 1307, I held a Synod right here in Cologne where we put their fondness for free love right at the top of the agenda. They claimed because they were led by the Spirit of God they were no longer subject to the law of the church. They said the law cannot be imposed on the just who worship the true God. I said, 'Is that right? We'll show you the law here in Cologne all right!' The inquisition has been after them ever since."

"That it has," agreed Leon.

"Were they not burned on my watch?" Virneburg said to Holzheiser. "Surely you have not forgotten the fate of Walter of Cologne and all his Beghard followers! You arrested them yourself! For twenty-two years I have been the Archbishop, and I have advocated the destruction of heretics from the first day. Did I not issue a decree calling for the dissolution of all Beguine associations and their integration into organizations approved by the Pope?"

"What I said about the Beghards and Beguines—. I did not mean to suggest you were remiss," Leon responded.

"It was the Pope who threw water on that fire," interjected Holzheiser, seeking further to mollify the Archbishop. "He should never have declared that the heretical Beguines resided in Italy while the benign ones lived here in Northern Germany—especially after your decree. It complicated matters, and we know ourselves that the Beguinages have always been infested with Free Spirits here in Cologne no matter what Pope John says."

"And their infestation continues," Virneburg said, placated.

"Yes, it was the Pope," seconded Leon.

"Pope John has always said that neither he nor any other Pope is infallible," Virneburg added. "To claim that the Pope is infallible is 'the work of the devil,' he said."

"He didn't have to worry about the devil in this case, then," said Leon. "John could scarcely have been more wrong. Were that you were in Avignon in his place. Heresy would have been eliminated as it was under Innocent III. That is what we must do today— mean business. Just as did Innocent with the Cathars."

"That is what I call meaning business," said Holzheiser. "There was a Pope who knew what he was about, not like our John. Though John is tough, sometimes it is not enough. You would not have these problems in Cologne with a Pope like Innocent, my lord. Those Cathars believed the world and all life was nothing but sin. Even procreation was a sin. 'All right,' said Innocent. 'You won't follow the high ideals of our holy church? Whisk! Be gone, foul detestable heretics!'"

Holzheiser swept his hand though the air as though he were swatting a gnat.

"They knew how to do it back then!" put in Leon. "They had this monk who to catch a Cathar made as if to seduce a young virgin. When she refused him, he knew she must be a Cathar. On interrogation the facts came out. She didn't believe in the congress of man and woman. They sent her to the flames quick enough."

"Where she well belonged," exclaimed Holzheiser.

"You don't hear much about the Cathars today," Leon said. "A few here and there we mop up whenever we find them. That's about all. History teaches us well. That is what we must do with all these mystical Beghards and Beguines and all their Free Spirit, free love ways. There is only one way to deal with a heretic who won't renounce. Total annihilation! Today that means burning!"

"Or drowning!" interjected Holzheiser, who sometimes felt partial to that method. "Innocent knew well enough how to extirpate that foul Cathar abomination, and while our Pope John knows it too—I would not deny him the credit he deserves—he knows it not so well as do you, noble Sir. Let us start at the top. And we know who is at the top of the heresy heap in Cologne, the one who is in such sympathy with these Beguines."

"Meister Eckhart!" hissed Leon with finality.

Virneburg took a seat and drummed his fingers on the library table as he looked back and forth from Leon to Holzheiser.

"What have you got on him," he said finally.

Holzheiser and Leon got up and moved their chairs nearer to the table to be closer to Virneburg. Leon sat down closest to him. Holzheiser leafed through the stack of papers before him until he found the one he wanted and handed it to Leon.

"The major charges are these," said Leon reading. "He has said that he is equal with God. Listen, these are his words. 'The eye with which I see God is the same eye with which God sees me. My eye and God's eye are one eye, one seeing, one knowing and one love.'"

"Virneburg frowned. "This is serious. But is it substantial enough? Will it stand up as a strong enough charge to merit a heresy indictment? I have doubts of this."

"I have much more."

"Read him another one," insisted Holzheiser.

"He expresses views such as that we should love our own sins. Well, not quite, but almost the same. He goes around saying it is possible to sin without regret. Does this not sound like the Free Spirits?"

"Are you sure of this?" asked Virneburg alarmed.

"Listen to his own words." Leon took another sheet of paper which Holzheiser handed him and read. "'If a man is rightly disposed he should not regret having committed a thousand mortal sins.' He writes this in German, not in Latin, and it is intended for the common people."

The Archbishop stiffened as he heard these words. "It is apparent this Meister teaches things to the people that could lead them into error. You could be right."

"It is not all my lord," Leon continued. "He teaches that we are one and the same with all creatures. The birds, the dogs, the stags, and wild beasts of the forest."

"What?" asked Virneburg with disbelief. "That is nonsense. Tell me more."

Holzheiser selected another piece of paper from his stack and gave it to Leon who once more began to read, with Holzheiser watching all the while the elderly Virneburg's growing agitation.

"'As flowing forth from God all things are equal. Angels, man, and creatures all proceed from God alike in their first emanation. Things are all the same in God. They are God himself.'"

"This is surely blasphemy," Virneburg said. "We humans, we are made in the image of God. The lower creatures can attain no such stature."

"It is also heresy," Holzheiser interposed.

"Let me just finish, my lord," continued Leon. "There is more. Here, you read it yourself."

Leon started to hand the paper to Virneburg, but Holzheiser reached over, snatched it from his hand, scanned it quickly, and began to read.

"'God delights so in this likeness that he pours out his whole substance into it. His pleasure is as great as if he were a horse turned loose in a lush meadow. Giving vent to his horse nature by galloping full tilt about the field, he enjoys it and it is his nature. So it is with God. It is his pleasure and rapture to discover likeness, and he pours his entire nature and his being in this likeness, for he is this likeness himself. God gives to everything alike.'"

Holzheiser slammed the paper down on the table and hammered both fists on top of it. "There! You see? God gives to everything alike? The beasts have the nature of God? Rubbish! Pure rubbish!"

Holzheiser bristled, his face beginning to turn red. "Is this learned Meister Eckhart not even familiar with our book of Genesis which states that man has dominion over every living thing? This Meister is in a position of leadership yet he leads our people astray! Enough is enough!"

Holzheiser cast his penetrating gaze directly at Virneburg as if to challenge any disagreement that might emerge. Leon quickly lowered his eyes. For hardly had his father mentioned the famous scripture in Genesis 1:28 than Genesis 2:15 leapt to mind. *The Lord God took the man and put him in the garden of Eden to till it and keep it.* The Lord intended that his flock should steward His other creatures, not subjugate them according to man's will in the manner in which some people interpreted Genesis 1:28. But Leon had no intention to debate his own father's argument by bringing Genesis 2:15 into the discussion.

All were silent. Holzheiser seemed satisfied and allowed his quick smile to surface for a moment before closing it down.

"It does seem our good priest is leading the people astray," Virneburg said. "We must prevent this. But if there is to be a prosecution, the question arises of who can prosecute a case like this? Who is even capable? You saw what Eckhart did against we Franciscans at the Paris debates."

"He covered himself in glory," Holzheiser agreed. "Who could forget that."

"And may the Dominicans be the worse for it," said Leon vehemently.

"We are not here to defend the honor of the Franciscans," Virneburg said coolly. "What I care about is what happened in Strasbourg where the Free Spirits were running free and loose everywhere. I do not want it happening here."

"We need Franciscans on the panel if we are to set up an inquisition," Holzheiser said confidently.

"Do you have someone in mind?"

"We could get Benherus Friso and Peter de Estate, two excellent Franciscans."

"Haven't I heard those names before?" Virneburg asked.

"They are experts in heresy matters."

"How experienced are they? Are you sure they can handle it?"

"We must have someone who can do the job," Holzheiser said. "I can think of no others, and they will draw up a list of errors that cannot be so easily refuted. Also, it would be good to appoint a prominent citizen from Cologne to the Tribunal to assist them. That will show our good faith and fair mindedness. We can require Eckhart to submit written responses so he cannot evade the accusations with his gifted tongue. We all know about his talent for words. We must force him to renounce. If he refuses he will get what every heretic deserves."

"Very well," Virneburg said. "I am agreed. I shall use my authority to make certain these gentlemen are on the inquisition panel. Now, as to the charges. I have not told you, but two Dominicans have already brought me a list of 74 errors against Meister Eckhart. Perhaps you know the gentlemen. Hermann of Summo and William of Nideggen."

"I know them by reputation," Holzheiser said, glancing at Leon. Word had gone around that Summo and Nideggen were out to get Meister Eckhart and were spreading stories for which they had no evidence.

"They may pose a problem, unfortunately. It seems some charges have been leveled against them. Lying under oath, inventing fake charges, something like that. I think this Hermann may have been imprisoned. I am looking into it."

"Their personal problems are their own problems," Holzheiser said, cutting Virneburg off. "If they have brought charges sufficient for investigation, that is what is important." Holzheiser stared at Virneburg to see if his argument had put the issue at rest.

"We shall see," Virneburg said. "We must make certain that all the errors of his teachings are set forth for inspection including his pantheistic leanings. We will take note that Meister Eckhart's teachings can lead simple and uneducated people into error. Central to our case will be the charge of heresy."

Virneburg lifted a small bell that sat at the center of the table and rang it. In a few seconds a page appeared.

"You rang my lord?"

"Have my butler go into my private chamber. He will remove my sword and crosier there from the cabinet and give them to you. Bring them hither."

While they waited, Holzheiser continued to leaf through the stack of papers producing different passages which he handed to Leon to point out to the Archbishop.

"Look what he says here!" Leon exclaimed. "'In every work, bad as well as good, the glory of God is equally manifested.'"

"Very disturbing," Virneburg said, shaking his head gravely.

"Well, look at this one," Leon gasped. 'Whatever God the Father gave to His only begotten Son in His human nature, He has given it all to me.' And look here at this one. 'God is not good or better or best. I speak ill when I call God good. It is as if I called white black.'"

"Words fail me," Virneburg said tautly. "It is good you gentlemen came today. I have wanted to attend to this matter in the right way for a very long time."

The page returned bearing an open case and placed it on the table. Virneburg waived him off. He bowed and quickly exited.

The case contained a very long ornamental silver sword and a golden crosier before which Leon, Holzheiser, and Virneburg stood deferentially.

Von Virneburg took all the papers on the table to a desk sitting in the corner of the chamber and then returned and removed the sword from the case. It was the symbol of the worldly power wielded by the Archbishops through the ages during the times when Archbishops held almost total authority in ruling the State.

Virneburg carefully placed the sword perpendicularly in front of him on the library table with the hilt at the top turned to the right. He played his fingers down the blade.

"This sword like Constantine's power represents the will of the State," Virneburg declared.

The Archbishop next picked up the golden crosier from the case, raising it at an angle so that the artfully crafted crook was at eye level. His eyes swept reverently along its shaft and back, starting and stopping at the crook. Both Leon and Holzheiser were fascinated, exulting in the sheer beauty of the work of art.

"I had this piece cast just four years ago in 1322," said the Archbishop. "Superb is it not?" Holzheiser and Leon could hardly disagree. Virneburg pointed out to them the enamel work on the staff detailing tiny delicate animals and falling leaves.

"See here," he said, pointing to the exquisite crook which was fashioned in the form of an angel. At the base of the crook sat a miniature figurine of Mary perched on a throne holding the baby Jesus. At her feet the figure of an Archbishop knelt with hands folded, glorious and dignified in his miter, his crosier lying on the ground next to him.

"Do you know who the Archbishop depicted here is?" he asked, looking to Leon and then to Holzheiser.

"Not you, Sir?" asked Holzheiser.

"None other. I sat for the effigy myself. Can you tell that it is me?"

"The likeness is unmistakable," said Leon, squinting so that he could see the small figure.

Holzheiser, who had put on his spectacles, leaned forward over Leon's shoulder. "Outstanding craftsmanship. A venerable likeness, my lord. It is a worthy piece."

Virneburg nodded with satisfaction.

"This golden crosier represents the institution of our church," he said solemnly. "It is the symbol of our authority and leadership. May it always remain incorruptible."

With the crook facing left and downwards, Virneburg placed the golden crosier across the sword to form a cross.

"In this manner, so do we backed by the Archbishopric invested in me and the will of the State form the cross of Christ. With this cross we do solemnly perform our duties. And like Constantine, may we always be victorious."

"Amen!" said Leon.

"I shall myself turn over the complaints against Eckhart to the inquisition after Friso and Estate have prepared them. They will also sit on the panel. If Eckhart is judged guilty we shall deliver him to the secular authorities who will force him to renounce his heresy. If he refuses, it will implement the secular judgments upon him."

"That means he shall burn like any other heretic!" Holzheiser said.

"Whatever shall be rightfully judged," Virneburg said.

The three men were silent for a moment and stared down at the crossed sword and crosier on the table.

"We thank you for this audience," said Holzheiser, while Leon gathered their papers together from the desk in the corner. "It has been a most important meeting and a noble work that we have done this day. You have handled this sensitive matter in a most tactful and professional manner."

The father and son bowed, turned and left the chamber. They walked down the marble corridors that echoed their footsteps and descended the stairs to the gardens below, pleased that they had accomplished their mission.

"It is a nasty business," said Holzheiser.

The pair proceeded into the gardens fragrant with flowers. They made a right turn onto a path of gravel and stones that crunched under foot, lined with neatly trimmed hedges that rose above their heads. The path led to the stalls where the stable hands were keeping their horses.

"Someone has got to do it," said Leon.

"In the years to come we shall see that we have taken the right course," Holzheiser said reassuringly. "Our forefathers would be proud."

Leon nodded his agreement. "We have followed in their footsteps. May God grant them his forbearance and peace."

In his palace the Archbishop Heinrich von Virneburg lifted the golden crosier once more and ran his eyes along its length, stopping to revel in the marvelous workmanship at the base of the crook illustrating him kneeling before the holy throne of Mary and Jesus with his crosier on the ground beside him.

Chapter 16
The Inquisition of Meister Eckhart

On September 26, 1326 Meister Eckhart produced his written defense to the inquisition panel against fifty-seven charges made against him by Benherus Friso and Peter de Estate.

In Meister Eckhart's chambers at the university Charles Egmund and Michael Altenbrenner read the defense and were ecstatic.

"This is brilliant!" declared Michael.

"You've made them look like fools," Charles crowed. "Look how you point out that if they condemn you, they are also condemning the church fathers who founded our holy church."

"I love this part," Michael said, and he began to read. 'The inquisitors object to certain statements of mine as false and heretical because they say that man cannot be united to God—contrary to the teaching of Jesus himself in the Gospel of John who says: 'Thou, Father art in me and I in thee, that they also may be one in us.'"

"It is like you teach, 'the eye with which I see God is the eye with which God sees me,'" Charles said. "And when you warn them they themselves might be guilty of heresy with these charges—. Oh that is good!"

"How I would like to see Virneburg's face when he reads that."

"They have tried to bury you, but they are left with their wheels stuck in a muddy rut," Charles roared.

"You have mopped the floor with them," Michael laughed. "It's almost as good as your debate with the Franciscans in Paris."

"No one could take on Gonsalvus back then except you, Meister. You were covered with glory just like today."

"Friends, come, come, I am not covered with glory," said the Meister, laughing with them. "It did not take much, not back then, nor today. With all their learning they do not know what God is or where he is. They can only pretend to know. But I am concerned. It is one thing to defeat these little minds. They have no real power. Virneburg is the one to watch."

"He is nothing beside you, Meister," said Michael.

"Let us not underestimate him. I cannot believe it has gone this far. That he should dare to drag me before these inquisitors? I who detest heresy and am one of the Church fathers? Why are they doing it? Have I not taught against the Free Spirit belief that people are free to sin if they are united with God? They tie me to such a belief because, as I have often said, we need not regret having sinned if we are rightly disposed."

"That only means that wrong can lead to right," Charles said. "That is obvious enough."

"Have I not always said there is right and wrong? They feel threatened because I would teach the ignorant to see. Did not Jesus heal the blind? Because they cannot comprehend the words and deeds of Jesus himself, they fashion these accusations out of their own limitations and refuse to reach more than an inch to understand what my words really mean. What must ultimately be judged is their belief in their unexamined dogmas and their refusal to widen their horizons. I have learned well here. There is almost no defense against them. You win, and they come at you again. You keep winning and they just keep coming undaunted in their ignorance, the depths of which has no bottom. That they should try to destroy the work of a lifetime on these trumped-up charges—. To fight them you must be prepared to vanquish them entirely. I understand now what Marguerite Porete must have felt when they burned her book."

"*The Mirror of Simple Annihilated Souls*," said Charles.

"That is the one," said the Meister. "No wonder she refused to answer their questions at her interrogation. They are too stupid to recognize ever that they are wrong. Well, I am determined. I shall continue to do my work come what may. Nothing can destroy that. And you two good friends, you will continue the work after I am gone. Tauler and Suso will do the same and everyone else who understands it. But we are forewarned. Virneburg is up for a fight."

* * *

131

It was raining hard when Holzheiser left his home for the Franciscan Monastery to answer the courier's urgent message that the Archbishop needed to see him immediately. The chill of the rain increased his bad mood. They had just put Meister Eckhart right in front of the tribune on a charge of heresy just like they wanted and still it had got fouled up. Couldn't anybody get anything right?

The abbot at the monastery greeted Holzheiser, took his mantel and hat, shook the rain from the garments, hung them to dry on a wall hook in the entranceway, and showed him into the lodge where Virneburg waited.

"I will be in the study if you need me," the abbot said as he withdrew.

"Your grace," said Holzheiser bowing to Virneburg.

"You have heard the news?" Virneburg began.

"I have," Holzheiser said contemptuously, hunching his shoulders up and folding his arms together. He was still cold from the rain, and he blew on his hands and rubbed them together before continuing. "He has made fools of us again. It is just like it was in Paris."

"It was not my fault. I was not there. It astounds me that Friso and Estate could have been so unprepared."

"Unprepared or was Eckhart just too good?" Holzheiser asked, irritably. "What further evidence do we need that he is a menace? Now he will be exonerated. There is nothing more that can be done."

"Nothing can be done?" Virneburg stormed. "No pantheistic priest is coming in here to pull a double cross on me. I don't care how famous he is! This is my court. I will tell you what can be done. I have already announced I will not drop the case. They are already flocking to Eckhart's defense, some prominent burghers and a few of his Dominican brothers like Nicholas of Strasbourg. The very same Nicholas who supposedly brought charges against him. I hear Nicholas will even send an official letter of complaint about our inquisition to Pope John. A complaint? After what he pulled? Who does he think he is fooling? It does not matter. I am resolved. Anyway, Pope John will see through that effort."

"Excellent! I was fearful Eckhart had escaped our trap."

"First we must discredit this Nicholas so that his judgment is likewise discredited."

"How do we do that?"

"He is trying to protect a heretic against a proper charge of heresy," Virneburg exclaimed. "That is heresy in itself. I will bring charges against him. Does he think that I cannot see through him? This is my city. And no heretics are going to run freely through it because some temporary Vicar General like Nicholas thinks he can go over my head. We took our authority from Constantine and crossed the sword of the State with the golden crosier. That is a solemn oath!"

"Well said, my Lord."

"What shall we do now?" Virneburg asked, suddenly calming down. He began to pace back and forth as Holzheiser watched with annoyance. "Don't just stand there!" Virneburg demanded. "Find a solution!"

"Why don't we bring new charges and force Eckhart to respond again."

"Oh, that's good for you to say. Won't he just pummel us on those as well?"

"Then we will make more charges. We'll keep going until we get him."

"An excellent idea and exactly my mind," Virneburg said, his confidence beginning to return. "But this time we must find some errors that are not so easily contradicted. I will make a list myself. You can do the same."

"Very well. We are agreed on how to proceed."

"Eckhart's Commentary on St. John is filled with errors. I am convinced of it. We can use that for a starter."

"Excellent! I'll get to work on my own list right away." Holzheiser bowed and exited the lodge.

Virneburg sat down at his desk and began to write up charges against Nicholas of Strasbourg. When he was finished he called his secretary in and asked him to bring him the Commentary Meister Eckhart had written on the Gospel of Saint John.

* * *

The Meister had seen it correctly all right. Virneburg was determined. This time he even claimed that Eckhart was connected to the Beghards and subpoenaed him to appear in person before his commission in four months' time.

Charles and Michael were stunned when they heard the news.

"What shall we do?" Charles asked.

"I have been thinking it over," said the Meister. "We must go on the offensive. When I go before Virneburg's commission I shall announce my decision to submit an appeal to the Pope in Avignon as is my right to do. I have looked into it. Virneburg is exceeding his authority. Only the Pope has the power to charge a Meister with heresy. When our appeal goes to the Pope we must hope and pray that he sees through all of this."

When the Meister appeared before the Archbishop's commission he brought an appeal with him and demanded that the Archbishop send it to Pope John in Avignon. But Virneburg was not about to let the Meister get off so easily. He was the judge in this case, not Pope John. Virneburg held onto the Meister's appeal for a month and then notified him he would not forward it to the Pope.

The Eckhart forces were stunned. The Archbishop had no basis for withholding the appeal. He could not prove his latest charges against Meister Eckhart and could not proceed further against him. Still the Archbishop refused to drop the charges.

"It is unbelievable," said Michael. "It will never end!"

But Meister Eckhart thought he saw an advantage.

"We now have him in a stalemate. There is light at the end of the tunnel."

The Meister described a plan he had devised. First he would announce publicly that he was not a heretic. Then he would declare that if any false statements were found in his writings he would retract them.

"We shall use Saint Augustine for our authority," the Meister said, watching for Charles and Michael's reaction. "Remember, Augustine himself wrote that a heretic is one who stubbornly refuses to be corrected. If I agree to correct any errors they discover, they will have no grounds for the charge of heresy. When they can find no errors, they will be put in their place and we will have been vindicated."

"I don't know about this," Michael cautioned. "Are you sure this is a good idea?"

"I am concerned too," said Charles. "They are sure to say they have discovered errors."

"But they will be forced to prove them. They cannot do it."

"They will come up with some connivance," Michael responded. "We should not trust them."

"What choice do we have?" asked the Meister grimly. "I know they cannot defeat this plan. It will reveal the truth, and it is a chance we will have to take."

* * *

On February 13, 1327 Meister Eckhart delivered a sermon to his Dominican brothers at the Dominican Church. Afterwards, Michael Altenbrenner read the Meister's proclamation asserting that he was not a heretic. He explained that the charges were the result of misunderstandings, that the accusations were false, that the Meister would take back anything he might have said unintentionally which was wrong, and, finally, that he would retract any fallacies anyone found in his writings.

Following his declaration, no one from the Virneburg side dared to come forward to meet Meister Eckhart's challenge. Who would be bold enough to go up against the edicts of Saint Augustine? If the Meister agreed to retract any errors that were found, there was no longer any grounds for the charge of heresy. Even so, Heinrich von Virneburg would still not drop the case. It rested in limbo for months.

In the meantime, the proceedings in the Eckhart affair made their way back to the papal palace in Avignon. There Pope John was deeply troubled. He did not like infighting among the clergy, especially when it involved an Archbishop. And it was an annoyance because it distracted the Pope from far more urgent matters. The papal troops were at war in Italy with King Louis of Bavaria. That's where the Pope's energies belonged. Now here was a case for which he had no appetite that demanded some kind of resolution. Moreover, Virneburg was the Pope's personal friend. And besides being a friend, he was an important ally in his battle against King Louis.

There was no getting around it. The Eckhart case would have to be heard. Pope John instructed his chief clerk to send Meister Eckhart orders instructing him to appear before a commission at Avignon. Then the Pope appointed a special council to sort out and consolidate the evidence. Finally, he asked Cardinal Jacques Fournier if he would examine the evidence to check for errors and offer his opinion.

* * *

At their shop on Bergstrasse Erich and Liese had been discussing the cloud of preoccupation that had settled over the Meister.

"He does seem more distant," Erich said. "He's as cheerful as always. But you can tell something is wrong. It started after all these charges were made against him. He said once I should take my notes to his assistants at the university if anything ever happened to him."

"It's a cloud all right," Liese said. "A cloud of heresy. It is like some uninvited guest has taken up residence in his mind demanding more attention with each passing day."

Erich perked up.

"When you say such things I know you shall become a writer," he said. "It is so—what is the word? Precocious!"

Liese went to her father and kissed him affectionately on the forehead. She knew he liked to encourage her as well as try out new words whenever he could.

"Look at you," Erich continued. "You are way beyond me already, my child. And you are right. That is exactly what has happened. It is all because of Virneburg's investigation. He has hammered relentlessly away, and now the Pope has stepped in. Why doesn't he mind his own business?"

"The Meister has to leave for Avignon soon for the trial," Liese said. "And we can do nothing."

"I wish it were in my hands. It's a terrible feeling to have no power when you need it."

In Meister Eckhart's quarters, Charles and Michael continued to hope as they tried desperately to figure a way around Virneburg, but they could not find a solution.

"We have one good factor on our side," the Meister said as he prepared to leave for Avignon. "The Archbishop shall not be involved in the Judgment."

"We can only trust that shall prove a blessing," said Michael.

"We must remain positive," said Charles.

"And ever vigilant," added Michael.

The two friends worried about the long journey the Meister had to make to Avignon. He would go in the company of several others, but the trip was more than 500 hundred miles, not an easy journey for a man the Meister's age.

"Do not worry about me," the Meister said. "I am unafraid! How often have I said to you, 'it is for a man to take everything that comes as if he had asked for it, nay, as if he had prayed for it.'"

"It is one of your favorite quotes," Charles said.

"Seneca's own words," Michael laughed. "Whatever you do, don't mention him when you reach Avignon! It's all they have to know that you're running around quoting heathens!"

The Meister chuckled. "We know, don't we, that truth is truth wherever we find it?"

Meister Eckhart looked around his quarters filled with books, papers and the memorabilia of a lifetime of study, meditation, reflection, and prayer.

"I feel like the heathen musician on his death bed who raised his head and exclaimed, 'O let me learn still more of this great art that I may practice it eternally.'"

The mention of death alarmed both Charles and Michael. The two friends started to protest, but the Meister stopped them.

"Do not fear the word death. It is only a word. Let us just remember, my friends, that when we are gone from this place we shall all be blessed more in eternal life by our power to hear than by our power to see. For the power to hear the eternal word is within me and the power to see will leave me."

The two assistants were captivated by the Meister's reflections and were silent.

The Meister saw that his words had accomplished their mission.

"Good!" he said, embracing Charles and then Michael. "May God's blessings go with you and may his will be with you and ready for your use always!"

"God's will" they repeated.

"I was outside a while ago saying good-bye to the garden and the flowers and trees I know so well, and yes, to the birds too. Let us never forget that not even the sparrow falls to the ground without the Father. If God cares for us, he cares for the animals too. Did not Jesus say it?"

"He did indeed," Michael said.

"Amen," added Charles.

"It looks like it's going to be a grand day to start a new journey. The wondrous blue sky is filled with sunlight and the magnificent clouds are drifting slowly by in all their glory. Fare thee well my good friends!"

Meister Eckhart turned and left his sanctuary.

Chapter 17
Death of a Meister

Once he got used to the idea, Virneburg saw the wisdom of the Pope picking up the Eckhart case. He had to admit the Meister was a clever one whom he had been unable to pin down. His offer to retract any errors was a brilliant idea and left Virneburg without the faintest clue of how to proceed. But now Eckhart was again within his grasp. Virneburg knew the Pope personally, a like-minded man who, when confronted with esoteric interpretations of the scriptures such as those made by this Meister Eckhart, brooked no nonsense. Like Virneburg, the Pope was a literal, practical man with his feet on the ground. This giddy fluff Eckhart fed the people had to be stopped. Besides, it was a threat to ecclesiastical authority.

In any case, the Pope owed him and owed him big. King Louis had defeated the papal forces in Pisa, declared himself emperor of Rome, and appointed Pietro Rainalducci of Corvara as the antipope. It was outrageous that the King even dared to think he was so powerful he could depose the Pope himself and replace him with someone of his own choice like Pietro. It meant that Pope John needed all the help he could get. And Virneburg was the Pope's most powerful ally against Louis.

Virneburg waited patiently for the verdict to come down. But the days and weeks rolled by with no response. Pope John was showing far too little interest for Virneburg's satisfaction. Finally, he could endure the tension no longer and wrote to him insisting that he make a judgment in the Meister Eckhart case. He had no doubt John would find against Eckhart and turn him over to the authorities in Cologne for judgment at which council the Inquisitor General Willard Holzheiser himself would preside. "Let the Dominicans see how they like that," Virneburg muttered with satisfaction.

Still another month flew by with no response. And then finally a courier came to Virneburg's palace one day with the letter he had been waiting for. His secretary brought him the letter and waited while Virneburg unsealed and read it.

"So this is how it ends," Virneburg exclaimed heavily. He handed the letter back to his secretary.

"Take this letter to my copyists and tell them to make a copy and send it to Willard Holzheiser at the Office of Heresy Investigations," he instructed. "Have them send it urgent."

"Yes my Lord."

The secretary took the letter and left the Archbishop's chamber. Holzheiser would get the letter in the morning, the same day on which he was scheduled to conduct a special ceremony in the high choir of the Cologne Cathedral. There he would honor the bravery of some of his elite guards.

The high choir had been dedicated by the Archbishop von Virneburg himself in the year 1322. He was glad it had been finished on his watch. It would take years and years to finish the cathedral, maybe centuries, but with the nave well under construction, the high choir could already be used for special ceremonies like the one Holzheiser would conduct the next day. Ceremonies and ecclesiastical functions—this was the work Virneburg preferred. As for all this miserable business with the heretics—. If only he could drive them all out.

* * *

Willard Holzheiser's grooms were just finishing dressing him in his vestments in the makeshift sacristy of the high choir in the Cologne Cathedral. It was one of those occasions in which Holzheiser, as a priest of the church, was required to wear his priestly robes. His son Leon and six other top investigators were scheduled to receive promotions for their bravery in arresting heretics and bringing them before the inquisition. As the Inquisitor General for Heresy in Cologne, it was Holzheiser's duty to conduct the ceremony. He would confer the promotions by dubbing each honoree on the left shoulder then the right, then the left again with a golden croisier as they knelt before him to receive the promotions. An officer from the Office of the Inquisition would read the citations.

The grooms lifted the sleeveless gold-embroidered, red, waist-length vestment over Holzheiser's head and over his full-sleeved white silk robe, fitted it snuggly around his neck, and smoothed it down over his trunk. Next they placed a pure white silk priest's cap decorated in gold trim on his head and handed him the golden crosier.

The head groom stepped back to admire his work. "You could not look more regal, my lord," he said.

Holzheiser and the retinue of honorees with Leon in the lead and Holzheiser in the rear left the sacristy and moved out toward the altar. They would proceed down to where a cadre of special troops were lined up in three rows in front of the high choir. The troops dressed in light blue uniforms stood at attention there waiting in readiness for the ceremony to begin. An audience of family members, inquisitor personnel, church clerics, and dignitaries from the community were also in attendance seated in front of the altar. The ceremony would take place in the middle between the cadre of troops and the audience. From their seats the spectators glanced expectantly in the direction from which the honorees and Holzheiser had just emerged into full view.

A courier rushed in, handed a sealed letter to Holzheiser's head page, turned around, and rushed out. The page glanced at the envelope, saw that it came from the Archbishop and was marked "URGENT." He headed straight for Holzheiser in a half run. Holzheiser saw the page approaching and stopped. Leon and the honorees also stopped and turned in the direction of Holzheiser as he took the letter from the page, noted it came from Virneburg and returned the letter to the page.

"Open it good page," Holzheiser instructed. The page broke the seal on the letter, returned it, and then retreated two paces to wait for further instructions. The letter was about the Eckhart affair. Holzheiser's hands trembled with anticipation as he began to read. Suddenly he stiffened, then returned the letter to the page.

"Have my secretary place it with the other important matters on my desk in my chamber," Holzheiser commanded.

The page bowed and retired.

"Meister Eckhart is dead...." Those were the words Holzheiser read. The rest was a blur. Dead? How could he be dead? Dead, when the trap had been set and was ready to spring? Dead, when the solemn oath of the State and the Holy Church were poised to crush the heresy out of his being? Dead, when he, Willard Holzheiser, the Inquisitor General of Cologne, had the blasphemous heretic in his invincible grip? Now, by death he had escaped?

Holzheiser brought his left hand up in a fist which he shook furiously. His jaws clenched tight, red infused his face like fire and with his right hand he brought the golden crosier smashing down on the hard, marble floor, creating a sound that detonated like a shot throughout the unfinished cathedral. Again, again, again, again, again and yet again he brought the crosier smashing down. The performance only added to his fury which he repeated and continued to repeat smashing the crosier down again and again and again. The sounds of violence exploded from the floor rising up into the ceiling where they reverberated like thunder in the open spaces between the vaulted gothic ribs the nature of which Erich likened to the skeleton of God and where Erich and Knorr had delivered with their own hands the mortar and stone that comprised its construction. The crackling sounds continued to echo on into the far recesses of the high choir, gradually fading away.

Holzheiser stood vibrating from head to foot with the honorees fearfully rooted in place. Leon took a step toward his father, but Holzheiser's glare froze him where he stood.

Suddenly Holzheiser began to cough. Slowly at first, but it rapidly increased making it difficult to breathe and he began to choke. He pawed at his chest, struggling for breath. Desperately gasping for air, Holzheiser dropped the crosier which clattered on the floor. He was strangling. Grasping the collar of the red and golden vestment with both hands, he stretched it out away from his body drawing in great gulps of air, but it was not enough and he continued to choke. Holzheiser pulled at the vestment around his neck twisting it frantically back and forth in an effort to get it off as he sank to his knees fighting death's grip. But the choking only increased and the coughing tore at his throat while tears flooded his eyes. He wrestled with the vestment ripping at it with his face turning purple. Foam and spittle bubbled through his lips as at last he got the garment over his head and flung it wildly away from him. He dropped to the floor in a kneeling position, wheezing for air, his cheek pressed against the cold, marble floor, his arms dangling limply at his sides. The inquisitor's pure white cap with the gold trim slid slowly from his head and lay beside his face alongside the golden crosier. The honorees kept their eyes lowered. No one dared to move. Leon looked desperately and tentatively around but did not know where to turn or what to do.

It was deadly silent except for Holzheiser's heavy breathing which gradually returned to normal. Slowly he got up, brushed himself off, wiped the spittle from his lips, and inhaled and exhaled deeply. He made no attempt to pick up his cap or the golden crosier or to retrieve the red and golden vestment.

The sun shone dazzling bright through the stained glass panels of the high choir as Holzheiser's tall, elderly, and nearly spent frame proceeded in rigid, faltering steps through the retinue of honorees toward the altar front where the inquisitor troops and the spectators waiting for the ceremonies to begin looked on in shocked wonder. Leon picked up the crosier and cautiously followed while the inquisitor honorees trailed behind. The disheveled Inquisitor General arrived at the altar place and glanced vacuously at the cadre of special inquisitor troops whose family members along with the audience struggled to comprehend the exhibition they had just witnessed. Leon handed his father the golden crosier and he and the honorees lined up as Holzheiser began to conduct the ceremony.

Chapter 18
Eulogies for a friend

Lillian and Candace had been living in Paris for two years working side by side with Friar James and Hugues de Besançon, the new Bishop of Paris. The Bishop loved to travel and had become totally dependent on his new Abbess, who, besides managing the administrative functions and working with him on the campaign against the oaths, assisted in arranging itineraries for his trips. He had just agreed to a visit to Cologne at Archbishop Virneburg's invitation to help him prepare for a major Synod on church expansion with the understanding that he and Lillian would still continue their work on the oaths during their stay. The Archbishop wanted to bring a Council of Bishops from all across Europe to attend. It was Virneburg's biggest project, and the Bishop and his company would all stay in the Archbishop's palace for several months making arrangements for the Synod.

The Abbess and her Assistant were excited by the chance to revisit their former home and see their old friends and colleagues at St. Mary's again. And it would be wonderful to see Liese and Erich and Kristen. They also hoped they might learn more about what had happened with Meister Eckhart. It was hard to believe that he had been put on trial in Avignon. Since then, they had been able to find out little about him.

Candace was busy working in the administration quarters for the nuns at the Cloister when she overheard one of the nuns talking about Meister Eckhart. Had she heard right? Was it the word "dead" that had floated across the room?

"What did you say?" Candace exclaimed, racing to the nun and interrupting the conversation. "Dead? Are you sure?"

The startled nun assured Candace she had heard the news only an hour before from brother Stephen who was as reliable as the dawn.

Though she rode no more than three or four times a year, Candace went straight to the stables, had a horse saddled and rode to the Hildegard Cloister right outside of Paris where Lillian had gone to sort out the speaker list for the Synod.

It was turning dark by the time Candace arrived. After she stabled her horse, she inquired about Lillian's whereabouts and learned that the Abbess was probably in the dormitory hall. She found her friend there seated at a small table talking quietly with another sister. Candles in the candelabras behind the table had just been lit and through the windows the remaining daylight was visible quickly dimming into night. Lillian glanced up and caught Candace's eye when she entered the room, but did not offer a greeting. Her look was enough to tell Candace she had heard the news. Candace took a seat beside Lillian who was speaking.

"They have won again," Lillian said. "Whenever there is a proud one who is so above them his presence threatens the outrage by which they live, that is the one they take down."

Lillian paused and introduced Candace to her host, sister Catherine.

"She is one of us," Lillian said. "She heard the Meister speak here in Paris many years ago and knows his work well."

"No one could forget the experience," Catherine said. "We had never heard anything like it."

Catherine sent for some tea and after they had been served the three women sat quietly talking.

"Let us go outside," Lillian said. "It is such a lovely evening for such bad news." Lillian got up and Candace and Catherine followed and together the three women walked out onto the lawn in the front of the dormitory and then out into a recently tilled field beyond the cloister that smelled fresh and clean from the newly turned earth. Silhouetted against the horizon, they continued their conversation speaking quietly into the night. The stars and the moon had come up and the boundless universe spread before them. If Erich had been with them he might have said, "there lies the true skeleton of God."

"The manner in which little ideas became invested with so much power that they become the master and the people their slaves is a marvel to behold," Lillian said "Now they have brought down the Meister. How many more will they bring down before the world opens its eyes to recognize that the little beliefs over which humankind struggles and fights so bitterly are nothing but that—little beliefs, little dogmas, little prejudices that wind themselves so tightly around the human spirit they sink it like a stone."

"It is a sad tale," Candace agreed. Though it had taken years, she was glad that Lillian had finally brought her over to the Meister's side. Now she could fully commiserate with her dear friend.

"We can only cling to our dreams and feed them to the world until it awakens some day," Catherine continued.

"That must be our goal," Lillian said.

"We must believe in it," Candace replied. "No matter how long it takes."

"What will you do now?" Catherine asked.

"We shall carry on as planned." Lillian said. "We will go with the Bishop to Cologne and stay at the Archbishop's palace there until the work is finished and then back here to Paris."

"The Bishop tells us it will take several months," Candace added.

"Candace and I will go back to Paris at least every other month for a few days just to keep pace with Friar James and coordinate our work on the oaths," Lillian said. "He'll have his hands full without our help when we're away."

"It will be good to get back to Cologne for a while," Candace remarked. "Paris can be gloomy. There was so much snow last winter."

Yet it had been magical when it snowed and fell into the gloom filling the grayness with its white.

"The trip comes at a good time," Lillian explained. "We will be able to help our friends Erich and Kristen get their daughter Liese off to Salerno. She will be studying at the university there."

"I have some contacts in Salerno who may be helpful if you need them," Catherine said.

"That would really be welcome," Lillian said. "Liese knows no one in Salerno and neither Candace nor I know anyone there either."

"I will put a list together for you."

"They will be saddened by the news in Cologne," Candace said. "No doubt they know by now."

* * *

In Cologne the news spread quickly. Erich was at the stationers ordering supplies when one of the book painters told him.

"What?" he asked in disbelief. How could it be? Not only did it seem improbable, when he inquired further, no one seemed to know anything about the circumstances of the Meister's death. People just said he was dead. That was it.

By the time Erich got home Kristen had heard too.

"Klauss the bookmaster came in to pick up his order," she said. "He found out about it last night."

"It is too mysterious. Does Liese know?"

"She was here when Klauss came in. She went off then to be alone. It's a bad time for such news when she is so excited about Salerno. It will be good when Lillian and Candace get here."

"They forced him to defend against these fake charges before the Pope's own tribunal," Erich said. "And they kept drawing it out. They were intent on getting him."

"Maybe the strain combined with the trip was just too much," Kristen said. "He was sixty-eight. It won't do us any good to wonder. I hope we'll hear more later."

"I'll take a few days off to gather all my notes together and get them in order. The Meister asked me to deliver them to Charles Egmund and Michael Altenbrenner at the university if anything ever happened to him. Who could have ever imagined it would?"

Erich paused for a moment and looked upwards. "Is it possible we are somehow in contact?"

"I would not know about such matters as that," Kristen said.

"Nor do I. Not knowing, I won't deny what is beyond our knowing. I'll just try to keep open to what is within. Who knows what waits there to be discovered."

"That is a full lifetime of work."

"It was he who taught us to learn to empty ourselves into nothing if we would become one with God," Erich said, putting his arms around Kristen. Not so easy to do. But what a change that has brought."

"Yes, he taught much that has changed our lives. We have been fortunate to have known him and he serves us still."

Chapter 19
Preparations for Salerno

It was almost time for Liese to go off to Italy to study in Salerno and she had been waiting days for Lillian and Candace to come to help her formulate plans. At last the morning arrived for their visit. Watching through the shop window she caught sight of the pair crossing the street toward the shop. Liese ran to the door to greet them.

"Dad is away and mom is upstairs," Liese explained as she showed the two friends into the shop. "It's so good to see you. I couldn't wait for you to get here."

"We came as soon as we could," Candace replied. "The Archbishop has had us working around the clock ever since we arrived."

"It's wonderful to be back in Cologne," Lillian said. "And you are looking fabulous. I adore seeing you again."

"The time is almost here," said Liese. "Soon I shall be in Salerno studying at the university. I can hardly believe it's really happening."

"I knew the Meister's recommendation would get you in," Lillian said. "And now he is not here to witness it."

"It is so sad. Mom and Dad cannot believe it."

"We'll have a long talk about it," Lillian said.

"The Meister and you and Candace. If you hadn't helped arrange this I wouldn't be going."

"We are the lucky ones," Candace said.

Kristen heard the group talking and came down to say hello. There was no need to mention Meister Eckhart—it was so apparent he was present in everyone's mind. She served tea and some apple and raisin tarts and then returned upstairs so that the three women could be alone to make plans.

"What an adventure this shall be," Lillian said to Liese, sipping the hot tea with pleasure. "And it offers the perfect excuse to come and visit. How I have longed to see Italy. It has been a dream since I was a girl your age."

"It's so exciting. I feel almost like I am the one who is going," Candace laughed.

Liese clasped her hands together, put her forefingers to her lips thoughtfully, and turned to look out onto Bergstrasse. Only a few pedestrians walked there in the early morning light.

"I shall miss everyone so much," she said, lowering her hands. "Especially Mom and Dad. And I shall miss you so much, my good Cloudy and Goldie Boy," she said playfully to her animal friends across the room.

Cloudy, who was lying comfortably in her favorite spot on the bench against the North wall, exerted herself just enough to open her eyes and then closed them slowly to a squint, settled back and purred contentedly. Goldie Boy, who was under the bench, looked up with expectant eyes, keeping them focused on Liese, and thumped his tail repeatedly against the floor.

Liese ran to Cloudy, picked her up and gave her a hug, burying her face in the cat's fur, then extended her outward so she could look into her eyes, and then hugged her again.

"I am so glad the Meister understood how precious you are," she said. "Just like I do. You are God's special gift to me and to the world. You too, dear Goldie Boy. Don't you worry, you two. Mom and dad will take good care of you until I get back."

"Let's get started," Candace said. "I have brought some travel documents you'll need. We'll go over your schedule first."

"And Sister Catherine in Paris has given us a list of people living in Salerno who can be helpful to you," Lillian added. "I've checked off the most important names."

Lillian handed the list to Liese.

"Even strangers are helping out," Liese said.

Lillian smiled reflectively. Her young friend's display of elation was a distinct sign that the doors to innocence that had slammed shut when she lost her mother might slowly be opening. But would she be able to dip into the comforting waters there or would the hard world where cruelty so often reigns leave its bitter taste behind forever. That was the question that loomed over Liese as she prepared to start her studies abroad.

"You can count on us, no matter what," Lillian said.

"Whatever happens," Candace seconded. "We will be there for you."

"How do things happen? Does it all come from above? Is it fate? Do we will things to happen from within? Do we just follow a dream, and if so, where does the dream come from?"

"Those are serious questions for a young women," Candace said.

"What shall I do? The questions just keep coming? Where are the answers?" Liese looked directly at Lillian.

"I can't tell you," Lillian responded. "If I tried it would ruin it all. Besides, my answers work only for me. You must find your own way. And that is the real answer to your question."

"That is just what I think," Liese said. "And oh! I am so looking forward to doing exactly that—just as soon as I get to Salerno."

Chapter 20
The Papal Bull

Nearly a year had elapsed after Meister Eckhart's death before Pope John XXII gathered some of the Cardinals closest to him together to make an official announcement of his rulings on the heresy charges against Meister Eckhart.

"I have sought advice from the Papal Commission on Meister Eckhart which even included such authorities as Cardinal Fournier who I am happy to have here with us today," the Pope announced. Fournier stood beside him and bowed slightly. "I have arrived at the following decision. I am issuing a Bull condemning fifteen Latin and two German works of Meister Eckhart's as heretical. I find eleven other Latin works as being dangerous and suspect of heresy. Because of Eckhart's declaration of February 13th two years ago, we are justified in saying that he recanted his heresy and so I have no need to render a judgment of excommunication."

"Was not the declaration issued more as a challenge to his Cologne accusers?" asked one of the Cardinals. "We do not know if Meister Eckhart would have agreed with our findings that his statements were in error."

This Cardinal could always be counted on to express an opposing point of view. Now the Pope seized the opportunity to show that he was an impartial administrator who took all sides of an issue into account.

"That may be, but nevertheless Eckhart said in his declaration if any wrong statements were made in his writings or sermons, he would retract them," stated the Pope emphatically. "Since we have judged that his writings are in error, we may safely conclude that he has recanted. It is why I am finding him innocent of personally being a heretic. There is no doubt, however, that his writings are besmirched with heresy and they are appropriately judged to be heretical. Meister Eckhart sought to know more than he should. We shall, therefore, now remove his teachings from the church so that they cannot lead anyone astray."

"So be it then," said the Cardinal. "It is well this matter is resolved, and justly."

"Eckhart was deceived by the father of lies, who often appears as an angel of light, into sowing thorns and thistles amongst the faithful and simple folk," said the Pope.

"Well put my lord," said another of the Cardinals. "That is heresy enough for the condemnation. I, too, am for it. Eckhart is fortunate to escape excommunication."

"Even if he is dead!" said another Cardinal.

"As long as we provide safe harbor for the peasants we know we are on the right track," Cardinal Fournier said expansively. "Their life is hard, and they do not need additional hardships imposed upon them."

"Words of wisdom, Cardinal Fournier," said Pope John. "You will be sitting on this throne one day yourself."

"If you want a jackass, be my guest," Fournier said, laughing modestly.

Chapter 21
The memorial service;
flight to Munich

"What do you mean they have found the Meister's work guilty of heresy?" the Abbess Lillian asked in disbelief. "How could they find his works heretical and claim that he renounced them when he is no longer here to defend himself?"

"It is true nonetheless," Candace said. "Guilty of heresy!"

"That is the last straw. Now it is time to fight back. I will arrange a requiem service in remembrance, and we will spread the word. Let all come who would pay tribute."

"But the Pope has condemned his work now."

"They shall not stop us," said Lillian, defiantly. "We will hold the service! We can do it at St. Mary's. My contacts are still strong there and I know the new Abbess well. This will put the authorities on notice that his work will not die."

"Very well. I will post notices. But we may regret this."

"Let us hope for a real outpouring of friends and supporters."

As soon as Lillian had made the preparations to use the facilities at St. Mary's, Candace sent out notices announcing that a memorial service for Meister Eckhart would be held in the main chapel at the Convent of St. Mary's, the same chapel in which Lillian and Candace first heard the Meister speak.

The program would begin with some choral works by the composer Perotin. A friar would read some selected passages from Meister Eckhart's writings and this would be followed by a short period of prayer and meditation. Lillian would speak a few words about the Meister's efforts to enlighten the peasants and describe his message of oneness with God. The service would close with another choral piece, this one a modern number by the young Guillaume de Machaut who was beginning to make a name for himself in the French courts as a composer and a poet.

When the day for the memorial arrived Lillian and Candace watched in vain for the large turnout they hoped for. Erich and Kristen were there along with Charles Egmund and Michael Altenbrenner. Langer, Knorr and Gretchen were also present along with Friar Horst, who Erich and Knorr had not seen since the day they met him at the Dominican Priory. Meister Eckhart's most devoted disciples Tauler and Suso came while Prior Francois traveled all the way from Erfurt. Sister Catherine traveled from Paris a few days in advance so that she could spend some time with Lillian and Candace before the service. The new Abbess from St. Mary's, a few nuns there, the Dominican brothers who had known the Meister well, and even some Franciscan priests also put in an appearance. But only a few faculty and lay persons from the university and parishes in Cologne attended. Liese was already in Salerno studying and had to miss the event.

Though Lillian was distressed by the modest showing, it could hardly have been otherwise. Those prelates, priests, monks and nuns who might have attended were aware that the Meister's work had just been condemned for heresy and that any support for Meister Eckhart would be seen as defying Pope John's authority. The peasants and other lay people did not come because they could not take the time off work to get there. As for the Beguine women who used to flock to hear the Meister speak, the inquisition had maintained an unrelenting assault on them beginning a decade earlier. That started after Pope John denounced the group yet threw their status into confusion when he distinguished between good and bad Beguines. They were soon loosely identified with the Fraticelli, a breakaway order of the Franciscans persecuted because of their strict belief in living lives of poverty, and many Beguines abandoned their dress and went into hiding. It was an intense period where public burnings of heretics flared up in Lunel, Lodève, Béziers, Capestang, Pézenas, Narbonne, Toulouse, and Carcassone. Beguines were also burned, and though the persecutions had ceased for the moment, the Beguines were still fearful and not anxious to draw attention to themselves.

"It is almost time to begin the service and there are many empty places," Lillian said, as she surveyed the chapel.

"Everyone is afraid," Candace said.

After the service, several of those who attended remained talking quietly, strolled absently about the chapel, or stopped briefly to speak a few words with Lillian. The spies who were present took careful note of the prominent role she played in the proceedings, including her talk in which she praised Meister Eckhart's efforts to educate the peasants.

Knorr saw Lillian standing alone for a moment and approached. He had been wanting to speak with her and introduced himself.

"I know that you gained much from the Meister. Erich has told me so much about you."

"You are the one who invited Erich to Cologne. We are grateful."

"It was my privilege. He is a close friend and I am always ready to help a friend. In the end I have been more than rewarded. And it also brought me here to this place right now all these years later. I want to know more about this Meister Eckhart. Erich has always talked about him, but I never paid much attention. Yesterday I met Candace and the things she said are remarkable."

"Do you have anything particular in mind?"

"Candace said Meister Eckhart taught that God is within us. She said the Meister spoke of God being one with us and we with Him. In that oneness a love is found that is eternal. Such premises astound me. But Candace insists they are much more than a premise. They are a reality that can be experienced. She said Meister Eckhart's work follows in the steps of Jesus who taught of our unity with God."

"If you like I will have some copies made of some writings I have done about him and send them to you."

"I would be grateful."

"Leave your address at the Chapter House and I will have it sent tomorrow. They will try to bury him now. But they cannot do it. They may succeed for a while. They may even keep him underground for a long, long time. But his work will continue because of people like you who are inquisitive and want to learn about it, and by people like me who keep it alive in our hearts and minds because we believe and experience it. Somehow it will get passed on to the next generation and the next and the next. I have faith that God will see to it."

"It is special to have had someone in life who meant so much to you."

"His words set me free like a bird which suddenly discovered its wings and what they were for."

"That is a good way to put it. Perhaps I, too, will discover this human form of mine has wings."

On May 1, 1329, a week after the memorial service, the Abbess Lillian was officially censured for suspicion of spreading teachings that had been judged heretical. She was ordered to relinquish her duties and report to the Office of the Inquisition the next day for examination by a panel of inquisitors at which Willard Holzheiser, the Inquisitor General for Cologne, would lead the investigation.

The Abbess Lillian of the Convent of St. Clare in Paris was seen for the last time in Cologne at the Archbishop's palace on May 2nd in the year 1329 leaving at the break of dawn in the company of another woman. When he was questioned the next day, a guard at the city gates responded that he had seen two women, one of whom may have matched the Abbess' description, riding out the gates at sunrise accompanied by two workmen who may have been peasants. The two women were dressed like Beguines and wore gray robes and veils. Though they aroused suspicion, the Beguines were no longer being persecuted in Cologne so the guard had no cause to detain them and let them pass through.

Lillian and Candace traveled to the safe haven of Munich where King Louis ruled and where the long arm of the church could not reach. They stayed there for a while, but then an almost obsessive desire to travel South to the land of blue skies and sunshine began to consume them. Soon they were living in Italy, the land of Princes.

Chapter 22
Heretics in the land of Princes

In Salerno Liese kept in close contact with Erich and Kristen and eagerly wrote about the fascinating events that were a part of her new life. Everyone hung on the news about King Louis' feud with Pope John, and Liese provided her parents with a running commentary.

In spite of his efforts to depose the Pope and consecrate Pietro Rainalducci as a new Pope under the name Nicholas V, the King did not succeed. Unpopular because of his tax levies, he soon left Rome to jeers and hisses taking the new antipope with him. Rainalducci began to move around, finally settling in the city of Pisa. There he lost his support base when he decided to break with the King. Meanwhile, Pope John had excommunicated him, and Rainalducci found himself having to live protected by a cadre of guards. His papacy was falling apart less than two years after it had begun. This was not what he had bargained for, and he soon applied for a pardon from Pope John which the Pope granted under terms that he accept honorable penance at the papal palace in Avignon from which he would not be allowed to leave the city. The Pope sweetened the offer with a pension of 3,000 florins. Rainalducci submitted, and that is where he was living even as Liese wrote. As for King Louis, though his dream of deposing Pope John had failed, he continued the fight.

Liese went on to describe other events in her new life in Salerno and hinted that she had been going out with a shy young man named Richard who was studying astronomy and loved to write poetry. Had she revealed all the facts she would have written that Richard was falling madly in love with her and hung on her every word. She did write that the previous evening they had gone for a stroll in the ancient Fornelle quarter with its small streets, alleys and archways where an Amalfitan community had once lived 500 years before.

"It was exciting experiencing the past," Liese wrote. "I think I'm starting to love history. Will that become my life's work? I'll write you soon again. And don't forget! You are coming here later this year. Dying to see you all. Love forever, Liese."

Also missing from her letter was the mention that Liese herself had begun to fall for the shy young poet with his head in the stars.

Liese did not mention Lillian or Candace in her letters to her parents either, though they had been living in Salerno for several months. They got in touch with Liese shortly after their arrival and the three woman met together whenever they could. But like Liese, they were also fugitives now, and Liese did not feel safe putting information about them in writing. The times were tense and informers for the inquisition were all around. If she had written about her friends, she would have mentioned that Lillian was working as the administrator for a large estate with Candace as her assistant. One of Catherine's friends had been looking for someone, and Lillian, with Catherine's recommendation in hand, arrived at the right time to take the job.

Liese often prodded Lillian into telling the tale of her awakening in the chapel at the Convent of St. Mary's in Cologne. She loved to hear Lillian retell the story.

"It was right after I heard the Meister speak that I began to wonder more about all the atrocities and injustices that I never dared look closely at before," Lillian said.

"You may be sure that I was quick to hear all about it," Candace teased.

Liese wanted Lillian to talk about how people who claimed they believed in God could participate in criminal acts like the Cathar wars or the burning of Porete, especially when they insisted they were answerable to God.

"How can these church leaders send down a reign of terror on innocent people and then strut around proclaiming their bravery? Look what they did to my mother and Walter."

"Their actions never cease to astound," Lillian said. "It is frightening."

"This is why I ask. Even at the university nobody talks about these things."

"The leaders appeal to some ideal to excuse their deeds," Lillian said. "And then they claim God is on their side. As long as you praise God you can do anything you want no matter how evil."

"I would loathe to be in their shoes," Liese said.

"That goes for me too," Candace agreed.

"Even so, there is hope for these inquisitors," Lillian said. "The Meister used to say that sin results when someone departs from blessedness and virtue. But he said the impulse to do wrong is never without use if we will only allow it to drive us to greater good."

"It sounds like Seneca," Liese added. "We have been studying him in philosophy class. He said that we are led to greater virtue through suffering."

"Yes, but look what they have done with the Meister," Candace said. "Will they learn greater virtue from that?"

"It was the judges' task to exercise the fairest judgment," Lillian responded. "They did not do it. Instead they relied on their tired old orthodoxy. That is what they must be blamed for, their rigidness."

"They won't admit their wrongs in a thousand years," Candace said.

"Well, they are just pitiable, those who cause harm and will not acknowledge it," Liese concluded. "Let us pray that they shall recognize they have lost their way and so come to greater good. How do we help them do that? That must be our task."

Lillian was impressed. "It is a privilege to be here beside you," she said. "Now tell me about your mother and father. Do they know that Candace and I are living here? They are coming to visit soon you say?"

I won't tell them about you until they are here," Liese said. "I don't want to take the chance of putting it down in words."

"You are right to be so cautious," Lillian said. "It is dangerous here in Italy just like in Cologne. We are thinking of returning to Munich. We can be safe there without worry, and I would like to return to working for the church."

"I'm surprised you ever came here," Liese said.

"It was an irresistible urge to fulfill a childhood dream."

"It is easier to ignore risk when you really want to do something," Candace added. "It would be almost impossible for Holzheiser to trace us here, so we felt safe coming. But even so, I feel danger all around. In Munich where we are safe we can at least express freely what needs to be done."

"Our job is to be a part of the truth in whatever way we can," Lillian said. "Truth has its own action. And when truth decides to act, no power on earth can stop it."

"In that we can take refuge," said Candace.

"I have begun to see that already," Liese agreed. "It is good to know there is always hope. And may the action of truth arrive soon. We need it so desperately."

Chapter 23
Epitaph for a Meister

Once Michael Altenbrenner and Charles Egmund recognized how meticulous and dedicated Erich had been in transcribing Meister Eckhart's classroom teachings, they enlisted him to help edit and compile the Meister's work for delivery to his disciples Tauler and Suso. Erich was glad for the opportunity, and a friendship between the three soon developed. Whenever Erich had any spare time he went to the university to help with the project.

One day Erich arrived just as Charles and Michael were talking over Pope John's bull condemning the Meister's work.

"It's just like I feared," said Michael. "They have used the Meister's declaration against him. He said he would renounce anything in his work they could prove was heresy. He can't defend himself from the grave so now they claim they have discovered heresy everywhere."

"What do you expect from a Pope who sees no further than the length of his arm?" Charles added.

"That's putting it mildly!" Michael exclaimed. "This pope is still trying to impose his views on everyone that Jesus and the disciples owned material things."

"He's been doing it for years," Erich said joining in.

"That's because the people want to know why the church and its leaders need so much money when Jesus and his disciples needed none," Charles said.

"They ignore his example just to get their own way," Erich said.

"Pope John has even demanded that his opinions about Jesus be taught in the universities," Charles said.

"If the Pope can twist Jesus' teachings like this it's small wonder he would condemn the work of the Meister," Erich replied.

"There was no need to condemn the Meister's work after he died," Charles added. "Pope John has done it just to appease Virneburg."

"How do you know that?" Michael asked.

"I would like to know that too," Erich said.

"Everyone knows that Pope John wants all German influence out of Italy and dreams of moving the papacy back to Rome. But how can he do it when this fight with King Louis is going on, especially after Louis stood before the people in Rome and proclaimed himself Emperor. John needs Virneburg's support in the battle against the King, and Virneburg wanted the Meister's work condemned."

"So you're saying it had nothing to do with heresy?" Erich asked. "The Pope just gave in to Virneburg's wishes?"

"Figure it out yourself," Charles answered. "Why did the inquisition indict the Meister for heresy when the usual remedy for clerics is to just censure them when the authorities want to put them in their place? Heresy is the most serious crime the inquisition can bring. It could have resulted in Meister Eckhart being burned at the stake if he had been found guilty and then refused to recant. The Meister's so-called heresy offenses hardly warranted this serious charge."

"What you say is very true," Michael put in. "But of itself, that still proves nothing. What evidence do you have there is more to it? The Meister did say things from time to time that sounded peculiar to many people. Things that were difficult to understand. We all know that. Some people could have interpreted them as being heretical."

"But he said nothing for which he could not provide a rational explanation," Charles said.

"That's right," Erich added. "And they are aware of that. They have plenty of evidence to exonerate him if they want. There is no need to disgrace him."

"You need better evidence than this to claim that the condemnation was nothing but politics," Michael insisted to Charles.

"Very well. Why did John not just allow the Meister's case to lapse like he did with William of Ockham? You don't see any charges of heresy aimed at Ockham."

"Ockham?" Erich asked. "Who is that?"

"You know, Ockham!" Charles replied. "The philosopher. He just happened to be in Avignon under house arrest by the Pope at the same time the Meister was there for his trial. The Meister, however, posed no danger to Pope John. Ockham, on the other hand—. Now there was a serious threat. He was out publicly denouncing Pope John everywhere he went. Called him a heretic. That's why the Pope put him under arrest. Ockham fled Avignon and joined King Louis. He now writes day and night demanding that the Pope be removed from office. John excommunicated him, but even with that he has still not condemned Ockham's work like he did with the Meister. And the Meister posed no more threat to the papacy than a grasshopper."

"So that's the way it is," Michael said.

"Exactly."

"Very interesting," Erich commented.

"And it is the same with Nicholas of Strasbourg." Charles continued. "Virneburg brought charges against him, but those charges are also being allowed to pass into nothing. If the church really just wanted to teach the Meister a lesson and put an end to some of his teaching, all they needed to do was make a simple censure like they always do. There was no need to bring him to trial for heresy."

"They wanted to humiliate him," Erich said.

"That's putting it mildly," Charles answered. "More like destroy him. Now they will try to bury his work so deep no one will hear from him again. That is what they hope to do."

"Well they do not have what we have," Michael said.

"Exactly!" Charles said.

"Yes!" Erich exclaimed exuberantly. "And they do not know we have it!"

"We must get the Meister's work safely to Tauler and Suso," Michael added. "They will know what to do with it."

"We shall see yet who has the last word," Charles said confidently.

* * *

In the years that followed, Erich often reflected on his last conversation with Meister Eckhart. He had written it down so that he would not forget. He was glad he had broken loose that day so the Meister could see for himself that his efforts had born fruit in him, Erich, the peasant from Gotha. The words Erich had spoken that day were pure heresy and he knew it. He could look out now to see that the failure of the church leaders to admit and recognize their own immoral conduct resulted from their failure to open the doors to the infinite God of whom they professed to be the representatives. This was the church which seekers like Lillian sought to reform by returning to the message Jesus brought to earth: Love of God; oneness with God; love for one's self; love and compassion for all humankind; respect and love for all God's creatures; goodness and mercy; and strength in standing up to evil.

The crime of heresy was the result of nothing but a great, plodding, and clumsy attempt to try to control the minds of the people. With power in their hands, the leaders used it to crush the spirit of the citizenry and trample underfoot anyone who would not conform to their narrow vision. To them, the universal spirit striving to achieve a system that benefits all the people, not just the privileged and the powerful, counted for nothing. Yet this was one of the central messages that Jesus taught in his mission on earth. This was what the rulers of the church in Meister Eckhart's day permitted to slip from view, indeed, if it was ever even present. Only the worship of a God they created and crafted in their own image out of their limited understanding mattered. If they had to force people to kneel to that image and take away their freedom to think for themselves in order to accomplish their goals, so be it. But they were the little church, vain, pompous, ignorant, strutting proudly about proclaiming their brutal deeds.

Through his good friend Meister Eckhart, Erich had found the big church. There, in His big church God is visible everywhere in all that lives, human and nonhuman, for He rules in His creatures supreme and, like the Meister said, gives to everything alike. Yet he also gave humans the freedom to act however they chose with His wisdom there always available to consult. For as Jesus, the one and only true leader of the church, clearly said in the gospel of Matthew:

"ask, and it will be given to you; search, and you will find; knock, and the door will be opened for you." And, as he said in John's gospel, "I am the light of the world. Whoever follows me will never walk in darkness but have the light of life."

Everywhere Erich looked, truth was there to behold. It was present in a blade of grass and a flower in bloom. It was present in the movements of an ant and in the cry of an injured animal helpless and alone. It was present in the kindness of a neighbor's eyes and in people who love and who are in love. It was there to be found in the life of the family and in the suffering to which all life is heir. It was there to be felt in the love that is everywhere manifest from which evil is overcome. It emanated from the words of Jesus as revealed by his disciple Thomas when Jesus said, "It is I who am the light which is above them all. It is I who am the all. From me did the all come forth, and unto me did the all extend. Split the piece of wood, and I am there. Lift up the stone, and you will find me there."

The time had come for the church of heresy manufactured out of human agendas and human misperceptions to give way and transform. The discernment of the spirit of Jesus through uncompromising reflection on the facts of who he really was by people of good will and hope needed to become the source from which a new church would emerge. This was what Erich and Kristen and Charles and Michael and Lillian and Candace and Liese and Catherine and Knorr and Gretchen and Francois and Horst and Langer and all the others sought to discover within themselves. There in the silence that surrounds, they could knock at the door of the unbounded, the unlimited, the infinite and the eternal which moves all things.

Biography of Meister Eckhart

Meister Eckhart was one of the most influential and controversial figures in the history of Christianity and the only priest ever tried for heresy by the Inquisition. He was born in the year 1260 in Tambach, Germany in the Province of Thuringia and died in the year 1328, probably on January 28th. A Dominican priest, Eckhart traveled widely to meet the needs of the church and the common people throughout his life. He was famous as a preacher and teacher in his own time and much revered for his sermons and talks which, contrary to the conventions of the day, he gave in the ordinary dialect so that the poor and the uneducated could understand his message.

Eckhart was particularly popular with women inclined toward mysticism, especially the Beguines, a religious order of lay women who lived communally, were often widowed, held their own services, and devoted themselves to worship and care for the poor and sick. The work of the Beguine Marguerite Porete and Beguines in Strasbourg and Cologne are thought to have influenced Meister Eckhart toward more "intensive vernacular preaching" during the latter part of his life.[1]

In 1302 the Dominican Order called Eckhart to Paris to study. There he participated in a series of debates with the Franciscans, most notably against the Spanish Regent Master, Gonsalvus of Valboa (1255-1313), who four years later would become the General of the Franciscan Order. Theology in the Middle Ages was prominent in people's minds in the manner in which politics is today, and the antagonism that existed between Dominicans and Franciscans might be compared to present day acrimony between Democrats and Republicans in the Congress. After a stellar performance at the debates, the Dominicans awarded Eckhart a Licentiate and Masters of Sacred

---

[1] Bernard McGinn, *The Mystical Thought of Meister Eckhart: The Man From Whom God Hid Nothing* (New York, N.Y.: The Crossroad Publishing Company, 2001), p. 9.

Theology. He was thereafter known as Meister Eckhart. The debates did not, however, win many accolades from the Franciscans who resented the newly crowned Meister.

Meister Eckhart was already sixty-two years of age when he was appointed to fill the chair of Albert the Great at the University of Cologne in 1322. Heretic societies were running rampant in Cologne at the time, and the Archbishop Heinrich von Virneburg tried to root them out, resorting even to burning their members. He especially feared the so-called Free Spirits, individuals who believed that their unity with God placed them above the laws of the church which gave them the right to practice free love. After some complaints came in that Eckhart was leading the common people astray, Virneburg and his Inquisitors, who were Franciscans and not fond of Dominicans anyway, zeroed in on Eckhart. They charged him with heresy in the year 1326. Meister Eckhart defended himself vigorously, and though the Archbishop could not find the evidence necessary to prove him guilty as charged, his enmity was now fully aroused. He brought new charges against Eckhart and would not allow him to appeal his case to Pope John XXII.

A friend of Virneburg, Pope John took over the matter in 1327, forcing Eckhart to defend himself at Avignon which was at the time the papal seat. It was during this period that Meister Eckhart died, probably on January 28, 1328. The exact circumstances of his death are unknown. He could have died in Avignon, or perhaps on the return trip to Cologne after his trial.

A year after Eckhart's death Pope John issued a Bull condemning several of the Meister's works as being heretical or suspected of heresy. The Bull further declared that Eckhart had recanted, a charge that was disingenuous at best, though it did give Pope John the means for exonerating Eckhart personally on the charge of heresy. So while Eckhart in death managed to avoid posthumous excommunication, the condemnation of his works effectively discredited them and, of course, Eckhart himself. His teachings were thereafter removed from the Catholic Church and he was disgraced.

Considering that many scholars, historians, and theologians agree that the condemnation of Eckhart's work was unjustified and taking into account the friendship between Pope John and Virneburg, the suspicion that some sort of collusion occurred between the Pope and his Archbishop cannot be avoided. Virneburg, who seemed determined to bring Meister Eckhart down, may well have needed an assist from Pope John.

Questions arise as to why Eckhart was the only priest in the entire history of the Inquisition to be put on trial for heresy, especially since other notable offenders of church doctrine, like the famous philosopher William of Ockham, were only charged with lesser offenses. Ockham, who was under house arrest in Avignon at the same time Eckhart was there for his trial, fled Avignon for King Louis' court in Munich where he took refuge and wrote extensively against papal authority. He even argued that Pope John should be removed from office on the charge of heresy. While Ockham was excommunicated after he escaped Avignon, his work was not condemned in spite of his attacks against Pope John. And he was never charged by the Inquisition with heresy, though his writings are considered to have been far more heretical and a threat to the church than Meister Eckhart's which posed little if any.

Another factor that cannot be overlooked is that Eckhart's trial came while Pope John and King Louis were waging war in Italy. Louis, who the Pope had excommunicated four years earlier, had just declared himself Emperor in Rome and the Pope badly needed Virneburg's support in his battle against the King. The stage was set for a quid pro quo.

In spite of the condemnation, Meister Eckhart's disciples, Suso and Tauler, and a few others managed to faithfully keep his work alive during their lifetimes.[2] After they were gone only a few others faithful to Eckhart's work, like Nicholas of Cusa (1401-1464), a Cardinal of the Church, remained to carry the torch. Without them Meister Eckhart would have entirely faded from view. Fortunately,

---

[2] The Friends of God, including the secular priest, Henry of Nordlingen, and the Strasburg merchant Rulman Merswin. See Richard Woods OP, *The Condemnation of Meister Eckhart*, published on Catholic Ireland.net, originally published in Spirituality, Saints and Great People (Nov-Dec. 2000, publication of the Irish Dominicans).

the publication of some sermons and tracts in Leipzig and Basel in 1498 and again in 1521 fanned the embers and helped the Meister's work survive until a handful of other theologians and mystics came along who understood the significance of his work. These included especially John Trittenheim (1462-1518), and Angelius Silesius (1624-1677). Silesius transformed some of Eckhart's ideas into poetry in his book *The Cherubic Wanderer*.[3]

The disinterring of Meister Eckhart really began when Franz von Baader (1765-1841), a religious philosopher, read a passage from Eckhart's work to his famous colleague Georg Hegel (1770-1831) in Berlin. Hegel was so impressed he immediately sat down and wrote a lecture on Eckhart which he read back to Baader the next day. "There, indeed, we have what we want!" Hegel exclaimed.[4] Following on Hegel's heels, the equally famous philosopher Arthur Schopenhauer (1788-1860) also discovered Eckhart. He compared him to Siddhartha Gautama, the Buddha himself, noting that "the spirit of this development of Christianity is certainly nowhere so perfectly and powerfully expressed as in the writings of the German mystics, e.g. those of Meister Eckhart...."[5]

In 1857 Franz Pfeiffer put together a collection of Eckhart's writings. Then in the 1880s Helmut Denifle, a Dominican priest, discovered some long lost Eckhart manuscripts in Latin in various libraries which Trittenheim and Cusa had referred to in their work. Other works by and related to Meister Eckhart have since emerged such as the Papal Bull condemning Meister Eckhart's propositions and Eckhart's *Defense* written to defend himself against the Inquisition's charges.

While Pope John XXII and Heinrich von Virneburg may have dusted off their hands in triumph thinking they had successfully dispensed with Eckhart von Hochheim, the work of his that has sur-

---

[3] *Meister Eckhart*, A modern translation by Raymond B. Blakney (New York: Harper & Row, 1941), p. v.
[4] Ibid, p. xiii.
[5] Arthur Schopenhauer, *The World as Will and Representation*, trans. E.F.J. Payne in Two Volumes (New York: Dover Publishing, Inc., 1969), Vol. 1, pp. 387 (http://digitalseance.files.wordpress.com/2010/07/32288747-schopenhauer-the-world-as-will-and-representation-v1.pdf)

faced to date reveals one of the most original minds in the history of religion. Today he is revered as one of the great Christian thinkers of all times, a brilliant teacher and spiritual leader.

During his lifetime Pope John Paul II spoke favorably of the efforts being made on behalf of Meister Eckhart. In 1992 the Master of the Dominican Order, Fr. Damian Byrne, formally asked then Cardinal Joseph Ratzinger (later elected Pope Benedict XVI) to abrogate Pope John XXII's bull condemning Meister Eckhart's work, a request that was never fulfilled.[6]

The church presently takes the position that since Meister Eckhart was not condemned for heresy, he can now be considered a good and orthodox theologian. While this is a significant improvement and his work is now in the public domain, Pope John XXII's Bull of condemnation on Meister Eckhart's writings that hovered over his work for the past seven centuries and stained his life in the process should now be nullified if the Meister's good name is to be fully restored. This should be done because it is the right thing to do. It is also a necessary step to assure that the full value of Meister Eckhart's life work is in no way hindered by an unjust judgment from the past. The position that Pope Francis will take remains to be seen.

---

[6] Richard Woods OP.

Printed in Great Britain
by Amazon